Other Books by
LEE BENNETT HOPKINS
Illustrated by
Vera Rosenberry

•

WITCHING TIME

A-HAUNTING WE WILL GO

MONSTERS, GHOULIES AND
CREEPY CREATURES

KITS, CATS, LIONS
AND TIGERS

Pups, Dogs, Foxes and Wolves

Stories, Poems and Verse
Selected by
Lee Bennett Hopkins

Illustrated by
Vera Rosenberry

Albert Whitman & Company, Chicago

Acknowledgments

Every effort has been made to trace the ownership of all copyrighted material and to secure the necessary permission to reprint from these selections. In the event of any question arising as to the use of any of the material, the editor and the publisher, while expressing regret for any inadvertent error, will be happy to make the necessary correction in future printings. Thanks are due to the following for permission to reprint copyrighted material listed below:

Genevieve Barlow for "The Fox and the Mole" from LATIN AMERICAN TALES: FROM THE PAMPAS TO THE PYRAMIDS OF MEXICO by Genevieve Barlow.

Coward, McCann & Geoghegan, Inc. for "The Sloogeh Dog and the Stolen Aroma." Adapted by permission of Coward, McCann & Geoghegan, Inc. from TALES FROM THE STORY HAT by Verna Aardema. Copyright © 1960 by Coward-McCann, Inc.

Curtis Brown, Ltd. for an excerpt from "Puppy" by Lee Bennett Hopkins from KIM'S PLACE AND OTHER POEMS by Lee Bennett Hopkins. Copyright © 1974 by Lee Bennett Hopkins. For a retelling of "The Dog Who Wanted To Be a Lion: A Jataka Tale" by Lee Bennett Hopkins. Copyright © 1979 by Lee Bennett Hopkins.

Library of Congress Cataloging in Publication Data
Main entry under title:

Pups, dogs, foxes and wolves.
    SUMMARY: An anthology of classic and contemporary
stories, humorous verse and serious poetry, and folktales
from around the world, all extolling the canine family.
    1. Canidae—Literary collections. [1. Canidae—
Literary collections.] I. Hopkins, Lee Bennett.
II. Rosenberry, Vera.
PZ5.P7897   808.8'036   79-253
ISBN 0-8075-6672-1

For Vera M. Egita—
who knows, loves, and understands dogs.

L.B.H.

Contents

Introduction: About Dogs

It's hard to imagine what the world would be like without the warmth, affection, and joy that dogs and humans bring to one another.

If you are like me, you forgive a playful puppy that chews your new sneakers, gnaws your parents' favorite chair, or shreds the newspaper which has your picture on the front page. You know this mischievous puppy will soon be a grownup dog—a dog that will welcome you when you come home, be your companion when you are alone, and protect you from danger.

In the United States alone, more than thirty million dogs are kept as pets, and about one out of three families owns at least one dog.

Some dogs are petted and pampered, but many work hard side by side with their owners. You've probably seen a guide dog acting as eyes for a sightless person or read about a heroic dog that has rescued someone lost on a mountain or in a dense forest.

Dogs as small as poodles and as big as St. Bernards have served in the armed forces during wartime. Large breeds, such as the German Shepherd and the Doberman Pinscher, are trained to protect their owners and guard factories, museums, and stores. For nearly twenty years, Macy's Department Store in New York City, one of the world's largest stores, has used Dobermans to patrol after closing hours. The four-legged guards have prevented damage by sniffing smoke and detecting the presence of thieves.

Dogs help people out in other ways, too. A Russian dog in 1957 became one of the very first living space travelers. On farms and ranches, dogs are taught to herd sheep and cattle. In the far north, huskies still pull sledges, and in some European countries, dogs are harnessed to carts. Swift runners, like whippets and greyhounds, are kept as racers, while hounds and terriers and spaniels are used to hunt. These dogs, with their keen sense of smell and their ability to obey commands, have always been good hunting companions.

Dogs are circus performers and sometimes screen and television stars, too. Your own dog probably performs at least a few tricks at your command.

The ancestry of dogs goes back to a wolflike animal called *Tomarctus,* from which wolves, foxes, and other doglike animals are descended. This entire family of animals is called *Canidae,* from the Latin name *canis,* meaning dog.

The dog was the first animal to be domesticated. Perhaps

twenty thousand years ago dogs accompanied Stone Age families, sharing bones from a hunt and sheltering in caves from storms and cold. The early Egyptians cherished dogs as well as cats. They bred greyhounds to hunt antelope, and one king, Amefta II, and his Pharaoh Hound were buried together in 2300 B.C.

Throughout human history, dogs have moved with people from one place to another, adapting to new climates and different kinds of work. In time, various breeds with different characteristics and abilities have developed. The Pekingese and Chow-chow are Chinese, while the Lhasa Apso is Tibetan. There is a hairless dog from Mexico, and a barkless dog from Africa. The Boston Terrier's name is a clue that this little black-and-white dog originated in the United States. Often these different breeds are suitable for specific purposes. For example, the long, slender German Dachshund was once used to hunt badgers.

Today the American Kennel Club recognizes over 120 breeds, divided into six groups: sporting dogs, hounds, working dogs, terriers, toy dogs, and nonsporting dogs. In size these animals range from the tiny Chihuahua, which may weigh only a pound, to the great St. Bernard, which may weigh as much as 180 pounds.

Purebred dogs, are, of course, highly prized, but they're only one part of the canine population. Dogs with ancestry that mingles many breeds—the funny, friendly, brave mutts and mongrels—are as loved and petted as the finest retriever or the

12

most pampered toy poodle. The dog that's your own is always the best dog of all.

Because dogs have been favorite friends for such a long time it isn't surprising to find many good stories about them. In this book, *Pups, Dogs, Foxes and Wolves,* you can read stories and poems about different kinds of dogs, real and imaginary, and their wild relatives, the foxes and wolves. Some of the tales are very old, and some are new, written by storytellers living today.

In Part One, "Dog Tales, New and Old," you'll meet the resourceful Wonder-Dog and other talking dogs, some clever and one not so smart. There's a story from India and another from Africa.

"Dogs Loyal and True," Part Two, has stories and poems about playful, devoted, and courageous dogs. James Herriot, the famous British animal doctor, tells how a nearly dead dog was saved by a bit of pretending. And then there are four memorable animals: Lucy and Mooneye, hounds that trail raccoons and opossums in hill country; Clarence, a maybe-hero; and Bimbo, a truly heroic dog, from the time when Mount Vesuvius rained fire and ashes on the ancient Roman city of Pompeii.

Stories and poems about the other members of the canine family make "Where Foxes and Wolves Roam," Part Three, both funny and exciting. There are old tales told in the southern part of the United States, in Puerto Rico, Peru, and the Russian Ukraine. Sam Savitt's "Dingle Ridge Fox" ends these tales with a tense, realistic account of hunting and being hunted.

Next time you look at your own dog or a friend's, perhaps you'll think more deeply about these beloved animals who give us warm companionship and have provided poets and storytellers with such rich and exciting ideas.

Happy reading!

LEE BENNETT HOPKINS
Scarborough, New York

Part One:

Dog Tales, New and Old

Puppy

We bought our puppy
    A brand new bed
But he likes sleeping
    On mine instead.

And I'm glad he does
    'Cause I'd miss his cold nose
Waking me up
    Tickling my toes.

Lee Bennett Hopkins

RICHARD HUGHES

The Wonder-Dog

There was once a wonder-dog, who belonged to a little boy.

Every day when he came back from school, the little boy taught his dog the same lessons he'd learned himself that morning. When the little boy set him sums, the wonder-dog worked them out in his head and scratched the answers in the sand with his paw, and he always got them right. In fact he learned to do almost everything children can do except one: he *couldn't* learn to sing.

Now in that same village there was a proud cat who had a very special tree which she wouldn't let birds make their nests in, because she thought nests looked untidy. "If I find you building your horrid untidy nests in my tree," she told the birds, "I'll tear them down and break all your eggs and eat all your babies! This is *my* tree—see?" And she scratched her name on the trunk with her claws.

The birds were sad, because this was far the best tree in that whole garden for nesting in. They twittered and chattered, but they couldn't think what to do.

"Somebody think of a plan," said a sparrow.

But nobody could. "We *can't* think," said a blackbird sadly: "We're too frightened of that horrid old cat to be able to think, that's the trouble."

17

"Well, if birds are frightened of cats, what are cats frightened of?" asked a thrush.

"They're afraid of dogs," said a linnet.

"Hooray!" said a robin: "That wonder-dog who lives in our village, I'm sure he would help."

"You go and ask him," the birds all twittered together.

So the robin flew down the village, and found the wonder-dog doing his lessons as usual with the little boy he belonged to. But when the robin started in at once telling the dog about their trouble with the cat, that made the little boy cross:

"Don't interrupt, you rude robin!" the little boy said. "If you want to talk to my dog you must wait till his lessons are over."

So the robin hopped up and down without opening his beak till lessons were done and the little boy had gone in to dinner. Then he told the wonder-dog all about the birds, and how the cat wouldn't let anyone build a nest in *her* tree. "So please come at once and frighten her," said the robin.

At first the wonder-dog didn't want to come: he was too grand to think that chasing cats was fun, like ordinary dogs do. "I can't come now," said the dog, "I haven't had dinner yet."

"Then come this afternoon," said the robin.

"I can't come this afternoon either," said the dog. "It's the little princess's birthday, and I've promised to go to the palace and show her my tricks."

"Then come this evening," begged the robin.

The robin looked so sad that the dog was sorry for him. "O.K.," said the dog, "I'll come as soon as I get back from the palace. Six o'clock at the latest."

"Promise?" said the robin.

"I promise," said the dog, and laid his paw on his heart.

Just then the little boy came out with the dog's dinner, so the robin flew back to tell the other birds all to be ready by six o'clock.

When the wonder-dog had finished his dinner, the little boy dressed him in his very smartest collar (which was made of bright red leather with shiny gold knobs) and sent him off to the palace by himself: "Don't dawdle on the way," the little boy said. "And mind you don't get run over!"

When the wonder-dog got to the palace they took him straight to the little princess's room. It was piled with birthday-presents almost to the ceiling, but she was rather a spoilt child and didn't care much about any of them. When he got there she was busy pulling the legs off all her new dolls. All the same, she seemed glad to see the wonder-dog. "Do you know how old I am today?" she asked him.

The dog didn't know, so he shook his head.

"It's a word rather like 'licks'," said the princess. "And rather like 'fix' and 'mix' and 'tricks'."

That made it easy, so the wonder-dog dipped his paw in the ink-pot and wrote a big figure "6" on the carpet in ink. "Clever!" said the little princess and clapped her hands. But then she rubbed the wet figure "6" with her foot to spread the ink on the carpet and make as much mess as she could. "You *have* made a mess!"

she told him nastily. The wonder-dog had meant to lick his figure "6" off with his tongue while it was still wet, but it was too late now, and he said nothing.

"What else can you do?" she asked him.

There were lots of other tricks the wonder-dog knew how to do with the little boy he belonged to. For instance, the little boy would say the name of a city or a river and the wonder-dog would point it out on the map. Or the little boy asked him questions, and the wonder-dog shook his head when the answer was "no" or nodded when it was "yes." But the little boy wasn't there, and you can't do that sort of trick with just any old ignorant little princess who doesn't know geography or arithmetic or anything much else. It would have to be something simple she could understand, so he started nosing about among the presents. He chose a policeman's uniform, a mouth-organ and a yellow tricycle. Then he put the policeman's helmet on his head and rode the tricycle round the room, blowing the mouth-organ as he went.

At first the little princess laughed, but she soon tired of it. "Get off!" she said. "That's *my* tricycle and I never said you could ride it. What else can you do?"

On the table was a vase of beautiful flowers. So the wonder-dog stood on his hind legs, picked up the vase with his two front paws and balanced it on his nose. Then he walked right round the room like that without spilling a drop. But the little princess threw a ball at him and knocked the vase off his nose so that it smashed on the floor.

"Stupid!" she said. "Now I'll tell my mother *you* broke it!"

It wasn't his fault of course, but the dog looked ashamed and sorry all the same (as dogs often do if you scold them, even when they haven't done wrong).

"I know," said the little princess, "let's play hide-and-seek."

So the dog shut his eyes, while the little princess climbed on the windowsill and wound herself in the curtain to hide. "Cuckoo!" she called.

To a dog, even little princesses don't smell exactly alike. They don't just smell princessy in general, each has a special princessy smell of her own. So even with his eyes shut he knew at once where she was, though he pretended not to and seemed to be hunting all over the room. When he let himself find her at last, "You *were* slow!" said the little princess. "Now sing me a song."

But singing of course was the one thing he couldn't do. "Woof!" said the dog.

"Stupid!" said the little princess angrily. "That isn't singing, that's barking. Sing properly!"

So the wonder-dog sat down with his nose in the air and howled, because that was the nearest he could get to singing. But this made the little princess even more angry. She caught him by his smart red collar with the gold knobs and dragged him into the next room.

"There's a piano in here," she said, "and you shan't come out till you've learned how to sing a whole song right through without any wrong notes!"

Then she slammed the door behind her and locked it.

The wonder-dog couldn't sing but he could play the piano all right—at any rate, simple tunes which he could hammer out with his paws on the keyboard. So he sat on the stool and started to play.

"*Sing!*" the little princess shouted through the keyhole. "You shan't come out till you sing!" But still he could only howl. "If you don't sing properly," she shouted, "you'll have to stop there all night."

The poor dog didn't know what to do. He would never be able to sing in a million years. But he had to get out somehow because he had promised the robin to be there not later than six o'clock, to help the birds by scaring the cat—and he'd heard it strike "Five" long ago.

He ran to the window, but it was fastened.

Then he saw a record player, and that gave him an idea. He looked through the records till he found a song. As soon as he had started it he sat at the piano, pretending to thump it and silently opening and shutting his mouth. Next time the little princess peeped through the keyhole she thought it really was him singing at last.

"I knew you could sing if you really tried," she said unlocking the door. "Before, you just weren't trying."

But when she saw the record player she was even more furious still. "You beastly cheat!" she cried, and tried to lock him in again. But the dog was too quick for her: he ran between her legs

and bolted helter-skelter downstairs. In the hall the Queen tried to stop him, but he dodged past the Queen. At the front door the King tried to stop him, but he jumped clean over the King. At the gate the soldier tried to stop him, but the wonder-dog tripped up the soldier and soon was right out of sight.

"I *must* keep my promise!" he thought as he ran, and sure enough there was the robin waiting for him.

"Quick!" said the dog, "They're after me." So the robin flew on ahead, and showed him the way to the garden where the other birds were all waiting too.

"This one is the cat's special tree," said the robin: "The one with her name on."

"Yes, but where is the cat? I can't stop long or the soldiers will catch me!"

So everyone started to look, but they couldn't find the cat anywhere. "She's bound to come back soon," said the robin.

But the dog turned round to be off, and at that the birds all started talking at once—like this:

All together
{
"Wait a minute!" sang the linnet,
"What's the rush?" asked the thrush,
"*Please* don't go!" croaked the crow,
"Be a darling," begged the starling,
"Stop a bit," chirped the tit,
"Wait while we look," cawed the rook,
"She's coming—hark!" sang the lark.
}

"But I can't wait!" cried the dog, putting his paws over his ears to keep out the noise of them all: "The soldiers will be here any minute!"

"Then we'll have to hide you," said the robin. "Just you climb up into the tree."

So the wonder-dog climbed into the tree, and the birds all worked hard building a big nest round him to hide him. Rooks brought large twigs, blackbirds brought straws, little birds brought feathers and wool, and swallows brought sticky mud, and they all worked together without any quarrelling till in no time they had built such a huge nest round him that he couldn't be seen at all.

"Sh!" said the linnet. "Quiet, everybody! I think I can hear the soldiers."

So the soldiers came and searched all over the garden, but they couldn't find the wonder-dog anywhere.

"He certainly isn't here," said the sergeant. "Come on, we must look somewhere else."

"What's that funny great bird's nest up there?" said one of the soldiers. "It's big enough for an eagle or something! May I climb up and see?"

"No you don't!" said the sergeant. "What will the King say if we waste our time bird's-nesting instead of looking for the dog?"

So the soldiers all went away, and just then the cat came back.

When she saw that huge nest in *her* tree she was furious. "Those beastly disobedient birds!" she said. "I told them they mustn't, and now they've built the most horrible untidy nest there I've ever seen! I must tear it down at once." So up she went. "If I find someone in it I'll eat him all up," she said.

"Grrr!" growled the dog, "you'll eat *me* up, will you?" And he stuck out his head with bared teeth.

The cat was so scared she jumped straight to the ground and rushed out of the garden with the dog after her. "Woof! Woof!" he barked as he chased her down the road. "You just wait till I catch you!"

"Help! Help!" miaowed the cat, too frightened to turn round and spit at him. "I never knew bird's nests had dogs in them, I'll never dare touch one again."

Just then she caught up with the soldiers. "Save me, save me!" she cried, jumping on to the sergeant's shoulder and rubbing herself against his ear.

"What a nice friendly cat!" said the sergeant. "That's an idea: if we can't find the dog, perhaps the little princess would like a cat instead."

So the soldiers took the cat to the palace and tied a blue ribbon round her neck and took her upstairs to the little princess. "What a *dear* little pussy!" said the princess, and gave the sergeant a chocolate.

Now that she was a royal cat, the proud cat was even prouder than before.

At first the little princess was kind to her, and gave her cream and stroked her. But soon she started being even horrider to the cat than she had been to the wonder-dog, because she was that sort of child. She spilt ink in the cat's milk, and rubbed her fur the wrong way. She pulled her tail, and even held her under the cold tap.

If this had been just an ordinary little girl or boy (like you) the cat would have scratched her as she deserved. But this silly cat thought you mustn't scratch little princesses, so instead she just looked at her with angry green eyes full of hate and twitched the end of her tail and sulked.

Now that the cat had to live in the palace and was never let out it was fine for the birds, they could build their nests wherever they liked.

As for the wonder-dog, he went back to the little boy he belonged to. He showed the little boy the trick with the record-player, and soon the wonder-dog was famous for his singing all over the world. But sometimes he wanted a holiday, so then he would come back to the garden and climb the tree and sit in his dog's nest and talk to his friends the birds.

Sunning

Old Dog lay in the summer sun
Much too lazy to rise and run.
He flapped an ear
At a buzzing fly.
He winked a half opened
Sleepy eye.
He scratched himself
On an itching spot,
As he dozed on the porch
Where the sun was hot.
He whimpered a bit
From force of habit
While he lazily dreamed
Of chasing a rabbit.
But Old Dog happily lay in the sun
Much too lazy to rise and run.

James S. Tippett

VERNA AARDEMA

The Sloogeh Dog and the Stolen Aroma
A Tale from the Congo

There was once a greedy man who through shrewd and sometimes dishonest dealings had become very rich. He was so rich in ivory that he had a fence of tusks all around his compound. He was so rich in sheep that he dared not count them, lest the evil spirits become jealous and destroy them.

The favorite pastime of this rich man was eating. But no guest ever dipped the finger in the pot with him at mealtime. No pet sat near him waiting to pick up fallen crumbs.

He ate alone in the shade of a big tree near the ivory gate of his compound. He ate much food and he became very fat.

One day as he sat on his eating stool, a procession of wives filed

29

over to him from the cookhouse. Each carried on her head a basket or platter or bowl of food.

Each put her offering before him and backed away to sit on her heels and watch him eat. This day among the delicacies were baked elephant's foot, fried locusts, and rice balls with peanut gravy.

A wonderful aroma came from the steaming food. It flooded the compound and seeped through and over the ivory fence.

Now it happened that, at the very moment the smell of the food was spreading through the jungle, the Sloogeh Dog was coming down a path near the rich man's gate. In his wanderings he had foolishly crossed the hot, barren "hungry country" and he was truly on the verge of starvation.

When the smell of the rich man's food met him, his head jerked up and saliva gathered at the corners of his mouth. New strength came into his long lean body. He trotted, following the scent, straight to the rich man's gate.

The Sloogeh Dog pushed on the gate. It was tied fast, so he peered between the ivory posts. Seeing the man eating meat off a big bone, he made polite little begging sounds deep in his throat.

Saliva made two long threads from the corners of his mouth to the ground.

The sight of the hungry creature at his very gate spoiled the rich man's enjoyment of his food. He threw a vex and bellowed, "Go away from my face, beggar!"

The Sloogeh Dog was outside the fence where anyone was free to be. He knew he didn't have to go away. But he had another idea. He trotted all the way around the compound searching for the pile of rich scraps which he was sure would be somewhere near the fence. He found not so much as a peanut shuck.

However, he didn't forget the wonderful smell of that food. Each day, at mealtime, he would come to sniff and drool at the rich man's gate. Each day the man would drive him away. And every day his anger grew until one day he left his food and went straight to the Council of Old Men.

He told his story. Then he said, "I want you to arrest that beggar of a dog!"

"On what grounds?" asked one of the old men.

"For stealing the aroma of my food!" said the rich man.

So the dog was arrested, a judge was appointed, and a day was set for the trial.

On the day of the trial, the whole village gathered about the Tree of Justice. From the start, the sympathy of the people was all with the Sloogeh Dog, for there was scarcely one of them who had not been swindled by the rich man.

But the judge was a just man. "I agree that the aroma was part of the food and so belonged to the accuser," he said. "And since the dog came every day to enjoy the smell of the food, one must conclude that it was intentional."

Murmurs of pity came from the crowd.

The Sloogeh Dog yawned nervously.

The judge continued. "If he had stolen only once, the usual punishment would be to cut off his paws!"

The Sloogeh Dog's legs gave way under him and he slithered on his belly to a hiding place back of the Tree of Justice.

"However," cried the judge, "since the crime was a daily habit, I must think about it overnight before I decide on a suitable punishment."

At sunup the next morning the people gathered to hear the sentence. They became very curious when the judge came leading a horse. He dropped the reins to the ground and left the animal standing where the trail enters the village.

Was the horse part of the punishment? Was the judge taking a trip later? He only shrugged when the people questioned him.

The judge called the rich man and the Sloogeh Dog to come before him. Handing a kiboko to the rich man, he said, "The accused will be beaten to death by the accuser!"

The rich man took off his gold-embroidered robe. He made a practice swing through the air with the whip.

The judge held up his hand. "Wait!" he commanded.

Then he turned to the people. "Do the people agree that it was the invisible part of the food, and therefore its spirit, that was stolen?"

"Ee, ee!" cried the people.

The judge held up his hand again. "Do the people agree that the spirit of the dog is his shadow?"

"Ee, ee!" they said.

"Then," boomed the judge, "since the crime was against the spirit of the food, *only* the spirit of the dog shall be punished!"

The people howled with laughter. Their feet drummed on the hard-packed earth. They slapped each other's backs and shouted, "Esu! Esu!"

The Sloogeh Dog leaped up and licked the judge's nose.

The judge turned to the rich man and, when he could be heard, he said, "The shadow is big now, but you must beat it until the sun is straight up in the sky. When there is nothing left of the shadow, we shall agree that it is dead."

The rich man threw down the whip, picked up his garment, and said, "I withdraw the charges."

The judge shook his head. "You caused the arrest," he said. "You wanted the trial. Now administer justice. And if the kiboko touches so much as a hair of the Sloogeh Dog, it will be turned upon you!"

There was nothing for the the rich man to do but swing the whip hour after hour. The people watched and laughed as the dog leaped and howled, pretending to suffer with his shadow.

As the sun climbed higher and higher, the shadow became smaller and smaller—and much harder to hit. The whip became heavier in the man's flabby hands. He was dripping with sweat and covered with dust stirred up by the whip.

When the man could hardly bear the ordeal any longer, the dog lay down. That made it necessary for the man to get on his knees and put his arm between him and the dog to keep from touching a hair. When he brought down the whip, he hit his arm.

The people screamed with laughter.

The rich man bellowed and threw the kiboko. Then he leaped to the back of the judge's horse and rode headlong out of the village.

"He won't come back," said the oldest Old Man. "He would get *his* paws chopped off if he did. He stole the judge's horse!"

The Sloogeh Dog slunk off toward the rich man's house, his long nose sniffing for a whiff of something cooking beyond the ivory gate.

Lone Dog

I'm a lean dog, a keen dog, a wild dog, and lone;
I'm a rough dog, a tough dog, hunting on my own!
I'm a bad dog, a mad dog, teasing silly sheep;
I love to sit and bay the moon, to keep fat souls from sleep.

I'll never be a lapdog, licking dirty feet,
A sleek dog, a meek dog, cringing for my meat,
Not for me the fireside, the well-filled plate,
But shut door, and sharp stone, and cuff and kick and hate.

Not for me the other dogs, running by my side,
Some have run a short while, but none of them would bide.
O mine is still the one trail, the hard trail, the best,
Wide wind, and wild stars, and hunger of the quest.

Irene Rutherford McLeod

Retold by

L E E   B E N N E T T   H O P K I N S

The Dog Who Wanted To Be a Lion
A Jataka Tale

Once upon a time a great lion lived in a golden den in the Himalaya Mountains.

Each day he bounded forth from his lair, looking north, west, south, and east until he spotted his prey. He then quickly made his kill.

One day he killed a large buffalo, ate until he was full, and went to a clear pool of fresh water to drink.

With enough to drink, he returned to his meal, only to find a wild dog feeding on the remains. The dog, knowing he could not escape, threw himself at the lion's feet.

"Well?" roared the lion, glaring at the dog.

"Lord of Beasts," the dog said, "forgive me. Let me become your assistant."

"Very well," the lion answered. "If you are a good assistant, you will feed on the best meat forever and ever."

The dog, feeling quite pleased, followed the lion to his golden den.

Each day the dog would step out and look north, west, south, and east until he saw an elephant or buffalo, a horse or deer. He would then go back into the cave and report his findings to the lion. In a loud, clear voice he cried out, "Shine forth in thy might, O Lord!"

At this, the lion bounded out of his den and killed the beast— even if it was an elephant.

As he had promised, the lion always shared his food with the dog.

Time went on. The dog grew bigger and bigger, fatter and fatter. He also grew prouder and prouder.

"Have I not four legs like the lion?" he asked himself. "Why should I continue to live as a lion's assistant? From now on, I will hunt elephants and other animals for myself. The only reason the lion is able to kill elephants and other animals is because I call out my magic words: 'Shine forth in thy might, O Lord!' I'll make him call out for me, 'Shine forth in thy might, O Dog!' "

The dog went to the lion and told him his wish, adding, "Please do not deny me this."

The lion listened and said, "Friend dog, only lions can kill elephants. The world has never seen a dog who can bring down an elephant. Give up your foolish plan at once."

But the dog would not change his mind. So the lion agreed, telling the dog to go and lie down in the den of gold.

The lion climbed to the top of a mountain. From there he saw an elephant in the valley below.

Going back to the mouth of the cave, he called, "Shine forth in thy might, O Dog!"

The dog bounded from the den of gold, gave three howls, ran down into the valley, and sprang at the elephant's throat. Missing his aim, he fell under the elephant's great, trampling feet. The enormous beast charged on, not even realizing he had crushed the dog.

Seeing this from the mountain, the lion sadly said:

> As a lion I was born,
> As a lion I must live,
> And as a lion I must die—
> There is no other way.
>
> As a wild dog you were born,
> And as a dog you would have lived,
> Had not your foolishness shone forth
> In all its might this day.

Part Two:

Dogs Loyal and True

Vern

When walking in a tiny rain
Across a vacant lot,
A pup's a good companion—
If a pup you've got.

And when you've had a scold,
And no one loves you very,
And you cannot be merry,
A pup will let you look at him,
And even let you hold
His little wiggly warmness—

And let you snuggle down beside.
Nor mock the tears you have to hide.

Gwendolyn Brooks

JAMES HERRIOT

Mrs. Donovan's Dog
from All Things Bright and Beautiful

Mrs. Donovan was a woman who really got around. No matter what was going on there in our town in the Yorkshire Dales of northern England, you'd find the little old widow, her darting, black-button eyes taking everything in. And always, on the end of a lead, her terrier dog.

I say "old," but she could have been anything between fifty-five and seventy-five. She certainly had the energy of a young woman, because she walked all around Darrowby in order to keep up with the latest events. Many people were upset by this, but her curiosity took her into almost every channel of life in the town—even veterinary medicine.

For Mrs. Donovan, among her other widely ranging interests, was an animal doctor. In fact, this part of her life transcended all others. She could talk at length on the sicknesses of small animals, and she had many cures that she used—her two important ones being condition powders and a shampoo of great value for improving dogs' coats. She had a talent for finding a sick animal, and when I was on my rounds I often found Mrs. Donovan standing over what I had thought was my patient while she gave it one of her own patent nostrums.[1]

"Young Mr. Herriot," she would tell people, "is all right with cattle and such like, but he doesn't know anything about dogs and cats."

And, of course, they believed her. I often encountered her, and she always smiled at me sweetly and told me how she'd been sitting up all night with Mrs. So-and-So's dog that I'd been treating. She felt sure that she'd be able to pull it through.

There was no smile on her face, however, the day she rushed into the surgery and cried, "Mr. Herriot! Can you come? My little dog's been run over!"

I was there within three minutes, but there was nothing I could do.

Mrs. Donovan sank to her knees. For a few moments she gently stroked the rough hair of the head and chest. "He's dead, isn't he?" she whispered at last.

"I'm afraid he is."

Later, she tried to smile. "Poor little Rex. I don't know what I'm going to do without him. We've traveled a few miles together, you know."

patent nostrum, medicine supposed to cure all diseases

"Yes, you have. He had a wonderful life, Mrs. Donovan. And let me give you a bit of advice: you must get another dog. You'd be lost without one."

She shook her head. "No, that little dog meant too much to me. I couldn't let another take his place. He's the last dog I'll ever have."

It must have been a month later when Inspector Halliday of the Royal Society for the Prevention of Cruelty to Animals rang me. "Mr. Herriot," he said, "I'd like you to come see an animal with me." He gave me the name of a row of old cottages down by the river and said he'd meet me there.

As I pulled up in the lane behind the houses, there was Halliday in his dark uniform. A few curious people were hanging around, and with a feeling of inevitability I recognized a small, brown face. Trust Mrs. Donovan, I thought, to be present at a time like this.

Halliday and I went into a windowless, ramshackle shed. There was a big dog, sitting quietly, chained to a ring in the wall. I have seen some thin dogs, but this one's bones stood out. His body was full of sores. His coat, which seemed to be a dull yellow, was matted and caked with dirt.

"He's only about a year old," the inspector said. "And I understand he hasn't been out of here since he was eight weeks old. Somebody out in the lane heard a whimper or he'd never have been found."

I suddenly felt sick, and it wasn't due to the smell in the shed. It was the thought of this poor animal sitting starved and forgotten in the darkness and dirt for a year. Some dogs would have barked their heads off; some would have become afraid and vicious; yet I saw in this one's eyes only trust.

"The owner's very simple," Halliday told me. "Lives with an aged mother who hardly knows what's going on either. It seems he threw in a bit of food when he felt like it, and that's about all he did."

I reached out and stroked the dog's head, and he responded by resting a paw on my wrist. There was a dignity about the way he held himself—calm eyes looking at me, friendly and unafraid.

"I expect you'll want to put the poor thing to sleep right away," Halliday said.

I continued to run my hand over the head and ears while I thought for a moment. "Yes, I suppose so. It's the kindest thing to do. Anyway, push the door wide open, will you, so I can get a proper look at him."

In the improved light I saw that he had perfect teeth and well-proportioned limbs. I put my stethoscope on his chest and, as I listened to the slow, strong thudding of the heart, the dog again put his paw on my wrist.

"You know, Inspector, inside this bag of bones is a lovely, healthy golden retriever. I wish there were some way of letting him out." As I spoke, I noticed a pair of black eyes peering intently at the dog from behind the inspector's back. Mrs. Donovan's curiosity had been too much for her. I continued talking as though I hadn't seen her.

"You know, what this dog needs first of all is a good shampoo— and then a long course of some really strong condition powders."

Halliday looked startled. "But where are you going to find such things?"

I went on. "Really powerful enough, I mean." I sighed. "Ah, well, I suppose there's nothing else for it. I'd better put him to sleep. I'll get the things from my car."

When I got back to the shed, Mrs. Donovan was already examining the dog despite the inspector's protests.

"Look!" she said excitedly, pointing to a name roughly scratched on the collar. "His name is Roy. It's a bit like Rex, isn't it?" She stood silent for a moment, obviously in the grip of a deep emotion.

"Can I have him?" she burst out. "I can make him better, I know I can. Please, please let me have him!"

"It's up to the inspector," I said.

Halliday looked at her in bewilderment, then drew me to one side. "Mr. Herriot," he whispered, "I don't know what's going on here. But the poor dog's had one bad break already. This woman doesn't look like a suitable person—"

I held up a hand. "Believe me, Inspector, if anybody in Darrowby can give this dog a new life, she can."

Halliday still looked doubtful. "I don't get it. What was all that about him needing shampoos and condition powders?"

"Never mind. What he needs is lots of good food, care, and love; and that's just what he'll get. You can take my word for it."

"All right," said Halliday. "You seem very sure."

I had never before been deliberately on the lookout for Mrs. Donovan, but now I anxiously scanned the streets of Darrowby for her, day by day. When she was nowhere to be seen the night the fat in the fish-and-chip shop burst into flames, I became seriously worried.

Maybe I should have called round to see how she was getting on with that dog. I had dressed his sores before she took him away, but perhaps she had needed something more than that. And yet I had a lot of faith in Mrs. Donovan—far more than she had in me.

After three weeks, I was on the point of calling at her home. Then I noticed her stumping briskly along the far side of the market place, peering closely into every shop window exactly as before. But now she had a big yellow dog on the end of a lead.

When she saw me stop my car, she smiled. I bent over Roy and examined him. He was still thin, but he looked bright and happy; his wounds were healed, and there was not a speck of dirt in his coat. As I straightened up, she seized my wrist with surprising strength and looked into my eyes.

"Now, Mr. Herriot," she said, "haven't I made a difference to this dog?"

"You've done wonders, Mrs. Donovan," I said. "You've been at him with that marvelous shampoo of yours, haven't you?"

She laughed and walked away, the big dog at her side.

Two months went by before I talked to her again. She passed by the surgery as I was coming down the steps, and again she grabbed my wrist.

"Mr. Herriot," she said, just as she had done before, "haven't I made a difference to this dog?"

I looked down at Roy with something like awe. He had grown and filled out. His coat, no longer yellow but a rich gold, lay in thick shining swaths over the well-fleshed ribs and back. His beautiful tail fanned the air gently. He was now a golden retriever in full magnificence. As I stared at him, he reared up, plunked his forepaws on my chest, and looked into my face; in his eyes I read plainly the same affection and trust I had seen back in that dark, dirty shed.

"Mrs. Donovan," I said softly, "he's the most beautiful dog in Yorkshire." Then, because I knew she was waiting for it, "It's those wonderful condition powders. Whatever do you put in them?"

"Ah, wouldn't you like to know!" She smiled at me sweetly.

PATRICIA LAUBER

Buried Treasure

Clarence was tracking. Nose to the sand, he was stalking a small sand crab. When the crab stopped, Clarence stopped and pointed. When the crab scuttled forward, Clarence followed. He was concentrating so hard that he didn't even notice when someone came over the dune and sat down beside Brian and me.

The new arrival was a boy we'd seen around. He was about our age, but he was much bigger than Brian. The boy said, "I'm Speed Armstrong. Who are you?"

When we'd told him, he looked at Clarence. "Is that your dog?"

"Yes," I said, "that's Clarence."

Speed hooted with laughter. "Clarence! What a name for a dog! Who ever heard of a dog called Clarence?"

"It's a very good name for a dog," Brian said angrily. "I bet you don't even have a dog."

"I've got something better," Speed said. "I'm building a rocket. As a matter of fact, you're sitting on my rocket site."

Brian and I looked around.

"I mean," Speed said, "when I finish building my rocket, I'm going to launch it from here."

"That's dangerous," Brian said. "You might blow yourself up."

"Of course it's dangerous," Speed boasted. "But I'm not afraid. I bet you're scared—and so's your dog. Any dog with a name like Clarence is bound to be."

Brian scrambled to his feet. "I'll show y—"

Speed paid no attention to Brian. "You should see Boy. He belongs to our next door neighbor, and he's a *real* dog. He's huge and he has great big bulging muscles that ripple when he walks."

"I imagine he's stupid," Brian said. "All muscle and no brain." As he spoke, he looked meaningfully at Speed's muscles.

"No, he isn't," Speed said. "He's very highly trained. All you have to do is say the word and he attacks."

"What word?" I asked.

Speed didn't answer.

"Yah!" Brian said. "You don't even know."

"Of course not," Speed answered. "Boy was right there while Mr. Gunn was telling me. If he'd said the word, Boy might have torn my arm off. Gosh, he's almost bitten the mailman, the milkman, and the boy from the grocery store. None of them will even deliver any more," Speed said admiringly. "Sometimes Mr. Gunn lets me take Boy out. I and he are the only two people who can handle Boy."

"Pooh!" I said. "Who wants a dog like that?"

"I do," Speed said. "When the Government buys my rocket plans from me, I'm going to buy a big dog just like Boy."

Brian and I looked at each other. Then Brian said, "I don't believe you have a rocket. I think you're making it up."

Speed laughed. "Well, I'm not going to prove it by showing you my rocket. All important rocket work is top secret. Nobody's seen my rocket and nobody even knows where I work on it, except Boy. Sometimes I take him along to stand guard." Speed looked back at Clarence. "What's he doing now?"

"He's tracking," I said.

"Clarence has quite a few kinds of very valuable dog in him," Brian said. "That's why he's such a good hunter and tracker. See how he points?"

"Points?" Speed said. "Dogs don't point with their hind paws. They point with their front paws."

"Most dogs do," Brian said, "because they only know how to point with their front paws. Clarence can point with any paw."

Just then the crab went down its burrow. Clarence began to dig furiously. Pretty soon all we could see of him was his hind quarters.

Brian said, "Clarence is a very good digger."

I said, "Clarence is good at everything."

Not to be outdone, Brian said, "In fact, Clarence is so good at hunting and tracking and digging that I'm going to use him to hunt buried treasure."

Speed howled with laughter and fell over backward. "Ah-ha-ha! That's the funniest thing I've ever heard—using a dog to hunt buried treasure."

"I don't see what's so funny about it," Brian said. "It's a good idea."

"That's all you know!" Speed snorted. "It's so silly that I'd bet my rocket Clarence couldn't find any buried treasure if he stayed here for a hundred years."

"All right!" Brian said. "We'll show you."

Just then Clarence gave up digging for the sand crab and trotted toward us.

For a moment, I almost wished Clarence was the kind of dog who bit strangers. But he loves meeting people, so he jumped all over Speed and licked his face.

Speed held Clarence off and studied him. "He's pretty small," Speed said thoughtfully.

"But very intelligent," I said.

"His tail curls just right," Speed went on.

"Right for what?" Brian asked.

"Right for fitting into my rocket. You've got to have a small dog with a curly tail—the way the Russians did."

I gasped. Even Brian was speechless.

Speed got up. "Be seeing you," he said and strolled off.

Brian found his voice. "Not if we see you first," he said, but Speed was gone.

That evening we went to see Uncle Matt and told him the whole story. Uncle Matt didn't think we had much to worry about. "Speed's a regular teller of tall tales," Uncle Matt explained. "Just last year he told everybody he was raising a tiger. Turned out to be a plain, ordinary cat that was tiger striped. Like as not," Uncle Matt said, "Boy is a Pekingese and the rocket's a burned-out firecracker."

We felt much better after hearing that. So Brian brought up the matter of hunting buried treasure. He told Uncle Matt about the bet. "I was just boasting back when I said it," Brian confessed. "But it does seem like a pretty good idea."

Uncle Matt didn't know of any buried treasure around these parts. But he suggested we talk to Mr. Tolliver. "He's interested in the history of the Cape," Uncle Matt explained. "Maybe he's turned up something in all those old books and maps he has."

The next morning we went to see the Tollivers. Mr. Tolliver agreed with Uncle Matt that our chances of finding buried treasure were pretty slim. And he laughed at the idea of Speed sending Clarence up in a rocket. "Why," he said, "it would take the U. S. Army and half a dozen top scientists to do that."

Mrs. Tolliver, though, was indignant. "The very idea," she said. "Imagine even joking about sending Clarence up in a rocket!" Then she went away and brought out a big bone with huge chunks of meat on it. "I was going to make soup from this," she said, "but I can always get another one. May Clarence have it?"

It was the most beautiful bone Clarence had ever had. He took it into the shade and began to work on it. He was still chewing by the time Brian and I were ready to leave. The Tollivers said Clarence was welcome to stay and finish his bone. But Clarence decided he'd rather come with us and bring his bone.

It wasn't easy going, for the bone was big and Clarence's mouth is small. Clarence kept having to lay the bone down and take a fresh grip on it. Brian and I both offered to carry the bone. But Clarence thought so highly of it that he wouldn't trust it even to us.

We were heading home along the beach when someone hailed us. There was Speed coming down the dunes. Beside him, on the end of a chain, stalked a huge dog.

Brian and I stood and stared. Clarence, who was standing near us, laid down his bone on the sand. Then he went forward, tail wagging, to sniff at Boy.

Boy snarled.

Speed tightened his grip on the chain. "You better keep your dog away," he warned.

Brian scooped up Clarence.

"Isn't Boy something?" Speed asked. "Did you ever see such a dog?"

At that moment, Boy lunged. Speed managed to hang onto the chain, but it didn't matter. Boy had seized Clarence's bone.

Clarence squirmed and whimpered in Brian's arms. "You give that back!" Brian said. "That's Clarence's bone."

"Tough!" Speed said.

"That's stealing," I said. "Mrs. Tolliver gave that bone to Clarence."

"I can't give it back," Speed said. "You don't think Boy's going to give it up, do you?"

"I thought you could handle Boy," Brian said.

"I can!" Speed insisted. "But there's no need to. My rocket's almost ready now. And there isn't room for Clarence *and* the bone." Speed strolled off with Boy and the bone.

We had to carry Clarence home to keep him from going after Boy. Clarence was very unhappy. We were unhappy, too. Speed hadn't been exaggerating. Boy was just as big and fierce as he had said. And this meant that he might be building an honest-to-goodness rocket.

When Aunt Jo heard what had happened, she gave Clarence a plate of chicken meat at lunch and promised him a new bone. Clarence soon cheered up.

Brian and I were still worried, though. And you can imagine what we felt like when Clarence disappeared. One minute he was poking around in some bushes. The next minute he was gone. We called and whistled, but he didn't come. We telephoned all the friends he might be visiting. But Clarence had vanished.

Brian was all for calling the police and having Speed arrested. I thought we'd better ask Uncle Matt first.

Uncle Matt listened to our story. Then he said, "Well, even if Speed wasn't exaggerating about Boy, that still doesn't prove he's planning to send Clarence up in a rocket."

"Then where is Clarence?" I asked. "He never goes wandering off for the whole afternoon this way."

"Please can't we call the police?" Brian begged.

Uncle Matt thought. "Tell you what," he said. "Suppose we start by calling Speed's family." He went to the phone. "Mrs. Armstrong?" we heard him say. "This is Matthew Gregory. Is Speed home? No, I wanted to ask him . . . What?" A look of concern came over Uncle Matt's face. "He did? No, Brian and Sis saw them this morning. Just a minute."

Uncle Matt turned to us. "Speed has disappeared," he said. "Boy came home alone before noon. But nobody's seen Speed since this morning. Where was he when you saw him?"

We described the place as best we could.

Uncle Matt repeated what we'd said. "All right, we'll meet him there." He hung up the phone. "Come on," he said to us. "Mrs. Armstrong called the police. We're going to meet Sergeant Wood on the beach where you saw Speed this morning."

The sergeant was waiting for us beside a jeep that he had driven along the wet sand. We told him the whole story.

The sergeant frowned thoughtfully and stared down the beach. "Did you think they were going to the secret rocket place this morning?"

"I thought so," I said, "but Speed didn't really say."

Uncle Matt had a suggestion. "What about getting this dog Boy to lead you to the place?"

"I tried that," the sergeant said, "but he just snarled at me and went back to sleep. He didn't seem to get the idea at all."

"Clarence could track Speed," Brian said. "If we could find Clarence, he'd find Speed. Can't we look for Clarence first?"

The sergeant grinned and ruffled Brian's hair. "We'll look for them both at the same time. Hop into the jeep and we'll take a drive along the beach."

As Uncle Matt, Brian and I watched for signs of Speed and Clarence, the sergeant told us that Speed's family didn't know anything about his rocket. What had started them worrying was Speed's absence at lunch. Speed might vanish for hours at a time, but he never missed a meal.

Sergeant Wood had hardly finished telling us all this, when Brian shouted, "Look, Sis! There's Clarence! I see him!"

Far down the beach a small dog was standing on the sand looking in our direction. The sergeant stepped on the gas. When he stopped, Brian and I piled out of the jeep. It was Clarence! He was perfectly fine except that he seemed a little tired. He also had something on his mind. As soon as he'd greeted all of us, he trotted off a few steps and then looked back at Brian and me to see if we were coming.

We followed him up the beach. The dunes here were very high. At their foot was a great pile of sand with some planks and beams sticking out of it. Clarence had spent the afternoon digging here. There were holes in the pile of sand, holes in the beach around it.

Uncle Matt and Sergeant Wood looked at all this. Then they looked at each other.

The sergeant said, "Wasn't there a hut here once?"

Uncle Matt nodded. "Belonged to some fisherman. Then in that bad storm two or three winters ago, the dunes shifted. The hut was swallowed up in sand."

The sergeant said thoughtfully, "Do you suppose—"

"Might be," Uncle Matt said. "I don't think the whole hut collapsed."

Looking very concerned, the sergeant hurried toward the remains of the hut. "Ahoy!" he yelled.

A faint voice called, "Help!"

"Speed!" the sergeant yelled. "You in there?"

"Yes," the muffled voice replied.

Sergeant Wood ran back to the jeep for shovels. Then, working with great care, he and Uncle Matt began to dig.

Clarence was delighted. He began to dig too.

In a matter of minutes, Sergeant Wood, Uncle Matt, and Clarence had made a big hole. Speed crawled out through it. Clarence went on digging as Sergeant Wood pulled Speed to his feet.

"You all right?" he demanded.

"I guess so." Speed was blinking and squinting in the light.

"Of all the fool things to do!" Uncle Matt said. "What did you do—blow the place up with your rocket?"

"No," Speed said in a small voice. "I couldn't. I mean, it wasn't a real rocket. It was just a model."

"Then what happened?" the sergeant demanded.

Speed explained that a few months ago he had discovered the hut buried in sand and tunneled into it. Part of the hut had collapsed but part was still standing. Speed had shored up the opening and used the hut as a secret place to keep his rocket. Everything had been fine until this morning.

"Boy found a bone," Speed said.

"He did not," Brian said. "He stole it from Clarence."

Speed blinked in Brian's direction. "Oh," he said, "are you here?

I still can't see in the light."

"All right," the sergeant prompted. "Boy had a bone."

"Well," Speed went on, "I didn't see what happened, but I guess he decided to bury it. I heard him digging near me. The next thing I knew the tunnel was collapsing and Boy was gone."

"Weren't you scared?" Brian asked.

"A little," Speed admitted. "But I knew Boy would save me. First he went away. When he couldn't get help he came back. He's been trying to dig me out for two or three hours."

"Boy!" Sergeant Wood snorted. "It's Clarence who's been trying to dig you out. Boy buried you along with his bone and then went home and forgot about both of you. If it hadn't been for Clarence you might have been here for a week before we found you." He took Speed by the arm. "Come on. Your mother's sick with worry."

Uncle Matt drove off with them. Brian and I said we'd walk home with Clarence. This time Clarence let me carry the bone, which he'd found shortly after Uncle Matt and Sergeant Wood had rescued Speed.

The next day Mrs. Armstrong came to call on us, bringing Speed. She wanted to meet Clarence and Brian and me and to thank us for rescuing Speed. Then she made Speed apologize for having said he was going to send Clarence up in a rocket.

Red-faced, Speed said he was sorry. "I was only teasing," he explained, squatting and patting Clarence. "I like dogs. I wouldn't really do a thing like that." Clarence took a nip at Speed's nose.

"Golly," Speed said, "Clarence likes me and I like him. We're friends. I wouldn't hurt him."

Mrs. Armstrong had brought Clarence a new collar. Attached to it was a little medal that read: CLARENCE—*for bravery*. She sent Speed to the car for a huge box, which he gave to Brian. It was a model rocket kit.

Brian didn't know what to say.

Mrs. Armstrong said, "Speed told me about your bet."

"But—" Brian began.

"Oh, I know," Mrs. Armstrong said. "You think of buried treasure as a chest of jewels. But Speed is my treasure."

Speed's face turned fiery red. "Aw, Ma," he said. "Cut it out."

For the first time I began to feel sorry for Speed. I mean, our mother may think Brian and I are treasures, but she'd never say so in public like that.

After the Armstrongs had left, Brian took me aside for a talk. Finally we decided to put the problem to Aunt Jo and Uncle Matt.

"I don't think I should keep the rocket kit," Brian said.

"And Clarence isn't sure he should keep the medal," I said.

"Gracious," Aunt Jo said, "why not?"

"Because Clarence had tracked Boy and was just trying to find his bone," I explained.

"And neither the bone nor Speed is really treasure," Brian added.

Aunt Jo and Uncle Matt said nothing.

"Mother likes us to be honest," I said.

Aunt Jo smiled at us. "I think you could keep them," she said.

"You must remember that treasure can mean different things to different people. Mrs. Armstrong would much rather have Speed than a chest of jewels. And Clarence would rather have his bone."

"Besides," Uncle Matt said, "you don't know that Clarence was just digging for his bone. He may have known that Speed was trapped. After all, he's a very intelligent dog."

That was certainly true. In fact, the more we thought about it, the more we began to believe that Clarence had been trying to rescue Speed. Anyway, that was the story printed in the town newspaper the following week. It had a big headline on the front page:

DOG SAVES LOCAL BOY

Then there was a long story about how Speed had been buried. It told how Clarence had tried to dig Speed out. Sergeant Wood told how Clarence had led the search party to the buried hut. Then Speed was quoted as saying what a fine, brave, intelligent dog Clarence was. At the very end, Speed said, "I'm going to get me a dog just like Clarence."

"Humph!" Brian said when he read that. "There aren't any dogs just like Clarence."

Dog

Black dog, white dog,
Yellow dog, brown.
Dog in the country,
Dog in the town.
Big dog, little dog,
Serious, clown.
Dog on its tummy
Or upside down.
Young one, old one,
Any one's fine.
Makes no difference
As long as it's MINE.

Margaret Hillert

BILLY C. CLARK

A Hunter's Moon

Jeb could tell by the warmness of the wind that it would be a warm and clear night. So clear and warm that Grandma Quildy feared rain. And when Jeb took the hunter's horn and strapped it across his shoulder and picked up the flashlight she cautioned him for the second time.

"Hunt low on the slopes tonight, Jeb," she said. "If it rains you won't have far to get to the cabin. I am afraid of the woods during time of storm. Don't stay out too late. Circle the slopes one time and then come in."

Jeb was so anxious to go that he didn't answer Grandma Quildy. He was happy to have a hound like Lucy to hunt with, and on such a clear night there was a good chance he might strike a coon.

He did not like to have Grandma Quildy warn him about the woods. He knew the woods well enough to name all of the trees, and almost all the sounds.

But Grandma Quildy knew the woods as well as he and this was why she had told him to hunt the slopes. She knew the danger of the woods during a storm. The tall trees on the ridge would be the first to catch lightning if it were to strike close to the mountain. During a storm there was always a high wind and trees were cracked and thrown across the path. During a storm was the time when the trees shed their dead or weak limbs, and one could hit you without warning.

Jeb walked to the outhouse and got an empty feedsack and tucked it in his belt. Lucy whimpered and sniffed around the yard anxious to get started, and the small pup ran after her trying to play. But Lucy would have no part of the pup. Once in the woods she would hunt the trail, her own trails, and it was up to the pup to keep her pace.

Grandma Quildy stood by the window and Jeb waved at her and started down the path. He followed the creek to where the path turned up the ridge and here he stopped. Lucy went into the beech grove and Jeb waited for her to circle. The pup followed her. Jeb knew that he would wait for Lucy to hunt a section of the ground. If she struck no trails she would come in. This would be a sign to Jeb to move along.

To the left of the path stood a gray rock, and in front of the rock ran a small creek. Under the rock was a good place for coon or

possum. If a coon was denned under the rock, Jeb figured he was probably out of his den by now, running the small creek searching for crawdads. The coon would probably work up the creek toward the head of the hollow. On the ridge there was a cornfield—a good place for coon.

While Jeb waited for the dogs to circle he walked over to the rock and flashed his light under it. He could see by her prints in the dust that Lucy had been here ahead of him. And beside Lucy's tracks were the tracks of the pup.

There were several holes under the rock and Jeb knew that each hole was a den. He dropped to his knees and reached his hand back in one of the holes. He picked up a handful of dirt and, holding it under the light, let it sift through his hand. Mixed in the dirt were long gray and white hairs. This is the den of a possum, Jeb thought.

The second and third hole belonged to a possum, but the fourth belonged to a skunk. The hair from this hole was black and white and coarser than the possum's.

None of the holes were worn slick, and Jeb figured they were old holes. And he had not really expected to find coon hair here anyway. He knew that a coon took to a tree den more often than a rock den.

The beeches near Jeb were likely to be chosen by a coon. Few beeches grew old and tall without having coon holes in them. And in these holes the coon would stay. Jeb shone his light into the tall beeches. There were several holes.

At some of the beeches Jeb stopped and shone his light on the bark. If a coon climbed the tree often, the bark of the beech would tell on him so. There would be claw marks on the slick, gray bark. Jeb found some marks on the beeches but they were mostly squirrel marks.

Lucy came back down the creek, the pup still with her. She sniffed again at the holes under the rock and started back up the creek. Jeb pulled the rawhide strap of the horn farther up on his shoulder and walked toward the head of the hollow.

Jeb didn't stop until he got to the top of the ridge. There he sat down on a dead log that had fallen across the path on his side of the cornfield, and waited for Lucy and the pup. In a short while Lucy came up the path behind him and he hissed her and the pup into the cornfield. Under the light of the moon he could follow them with his eyes to the edge of the cornfield. Behind Lucy, with his nose to the ground, went the small pup. Lucy stopped, sniffed, and then disappeared.

It seemed to Jeb that he had been sitting on the log a long time. Lucy had stayed out longer than usual. Jeb sat and listened to the wind in the trees. Now and then a bird fluttered from a tree into the darkness and each time Jeb jumped, thinking that Lucy was coming in. But each time when Lucy did not come he knew that the bird had probably been pushed from the limb by another bird and would have to find a new roost.

Jeb listened to the weird sounds of the woods. There was the hoot of an owl from over in the hollow. And from somewhere along the creek came the sound of a whippoorwill. Jeb liked to listen to the whippoorwill. Its voice was soft and clear. But not the owl's. Its hoot brought a loneliness to the woods.

A gust of wind swept across the ridge and Jeb listened to the sound in the trees. And then the wind died and the woods were quiet. Almost too quiet, Jeb thought.

Once, he wished that the pup would come in so that he'd have company. Jeb had not thought he would stay out this long. But it would be wrong to call the pup in. And he couldn't call Lucy even if he wanted to. She would only come to the sound of the horn if she were out tracking.

The wind became harder in the trees and still Lucy did not come. Jeb got up to stretch his legs and walked to the edge of the cornfield. The moon was overhead and was so bright that Jeb didn't have to use the flashlight to see the path. Lucy had been gone too long, he thought. He let his hand slide along the smooth horn and he touched the mouthpiece. Then he let his hand fall to his side.

Then, in the stillness of the woods, Jeb heard it. It was Lucy's voice. Loud and clear it sounded through the woods and bounced against the side of the valleys. Jeb jumped with joy and listened. Lucy bawled again and again, each time from a different place. They were short, quick bawls and Jeb knew she was trailing. Whatever she had struck was not far away.

Jeb waited to hear the voice of the pup. But there was only Lucy's voice. The pup is a silent trailer, Jeb thought. And he frowned. Jeb liked to listen to a hound that opened on the trail, first with short, quick barks and then a steady bawl when it had treed the game. To him this was the prettiest of all music. A silent trailer would only bark after it had treed, and some would not bark then.

Jeb listened to Lucy as she trailed the side of the slope and crossed a ridge into another hollow. She came out of the hollow and down a ridge. If she trailed over this ridge, Jeb knew she would be in Hurricane Hollow. Hurricane Hollow was a short hollow. At the head of it stood a large rock cliff. If Lucy could turn the game into this hollow and press it close enough, she could run it into the rock. Here it would have to turn and make its stand. If it was a fighting animal, like a coon, it would make a stand and fight.

Lucy's voice stopped. Then after a short while Jeb heard her open again. She had circled back to the valley. And then her voice sounded farther and farther away until Jeb had to listen close to hear it.

A loud scream came from the far ridge and cold chills swept Jeb's body. He looked into the darkness, toward the far ridge. Then he heard the scream again. At first, Jeb had not been sure. But now he knew the sound. Only once before had he ever heard it. He had been with Jeptha, and Jeptha had told him never to forget it. This was the scream of a wildcat. This was the deadliest of all the game a hound could hunt here in the mountains. It was not often that a hound would stand against one and fight. And most of the hounds that did were either buried or left somewhere on the mountainside, never to be found.

Lucy bawled, and Jeb knew she was following a slow trail. And this was the mark of a good hound. There would be no hurry for Lucy. She would trail slowly, but always moving closer to her game. A fast hound would many times overrun the trail and have to drop back and pick it up again.

The wildcat screamed again and Jeb thought it was egging Lucy on. It was on the far ridge, the ridge that turned into Hurricane Hollow. Jeb thought it would wait until Lucy worked closer and then would turn down the ridge—not into the hollow where it would be trapped. The wildcat must know, Jeb thought, that Lucy was a slow trailer. There was a chance that a fast hound could turn the wildcat into the hollow and force it against the cliff. And against the cliff the wildcat would turn and fight.

Other than its loud scream that seemed to stop all the other sounds of the woods, Jeb was glad it was a wildcat. He loved to hear Lucy bark and he knew on the slow trail she would run all night. That is, if she were not called off. And he couldn't blow the horn.

He was glad in one way he couldn't blow the horn. He could stay on the mountaintop all night and he would be able to tell Grandma Quildy what had happened. Even Grandma Quildy knew that a hunter never left the mountain without his hound.

Jeb found himself a soft place to sit on and started to sit down. Then he jumped to his feet.

Along the far ridge drifted the bawl of another hound. At first Jeb thought it was the voice of Lucy, clear and deep. But the long bawls instead of the short, quick ones told him it wasn't. Other than this, the voice was the same.

Deep and mellow the voice rang through the woods as though it were coming from a hollow log. It was hard to believe that another hound could have a voice so close to Lucy's. And then chills covered his body. He thought of the pup. There was a chance, Jeb knew, that the pup, being young on the trail, had heard the scream of the wildcat and had turned toward it, following sound instead of track.

Jeb caught his breath and listened to the steady bawl. He knew now it was the pup. And he was moving fast along the mountainside. So fast that he was sure to turn the wildcat into Hurricane Hollow. The wildcat screamed again, egging the young pup on, Jeb thought.

Once in the hollow the ground would be cleared by the small creek that came out of it, and the pup would move faster toward the cliff. Once against the cliff, the wildcat would turn. The pup would not have a chance. And yet, the pup had no way of knowing the danger of the wildcat. He was only following the sound.

From two hollows away came the voice of Lucy. For the first time that Jeb could ever remember, Lucy had lost the trail and circled back to pick it up. And into the hollow went the pup.

Jeb thought of the pup pushing the wildcat against the rock cliff, and then being torn to pieces by its sharp teeth and long claws. He thought of the pup sticking his head into the air and bawling to let Jeb know that he was a hound and was pushing his game. And that he had no fear of the wildcat. With the blind eye and stub tail he would face the wildcat, the deadliest of all the game here in the mountains.

Tears came to Jeb's eyes. And he called as loud as he could.

"Mooneye!" he yelled. But his voice died in the deep woods.

Jeb called again, and this time he started to run through the trees toward the ridge. His only chance was to try and catch the pup before he reached the cliff. Jeb fell into the thick underbrush and got to his feet. Tree limbs hit him in the face and brought more tears to his eyes. And the horn, swinging back and forth at his side, caught on low bushes and slowed him up. He pulled the horn from his shoulder and held it in his hand, crossing the ridge and into the hollow.

Jeb stopped to catch a short breath and listen. Behind him was the voice of Lucy, working the slow trail. By the time she reaches the cliff, Jeb thought, the pup will be killed.

Again and again the pup bawled, each time nearer the rock. In the hollow Jeb slipped on the slick stems of the wild fern and fell against the side of a large beech. The horn flew from his hand and into the air. Jeb wiped his eyes and found the horn. He yelled again for the pup and headed for the cliff.

Close to the cliff Jeb stopped. Against the rock, its fur bristling, stood the wildcat. In front of the wildcat, his head low, stood the pup. He was not moving in, as Jeb had thought he would, but was baying the wildcat, staying at a safe distance but close enough to press the wildcat against the rock.

Jeb was afraid to call. If the pup knew he was this close, the sound of his voice might encourage it to move in on the wildcat. Jeb stood, tears streaming down his face, the horn hanging limp in his hand. Beneath the moon he could see the stub tail of the pup moving back and forth. His head was turned to one side as if he were favoring the white eye. Then Jeb looked into the red eyes of the wildcat. He could hear the growl and see the sharp, white teeth. Lucy sounded again, closer, but not close enough. She was coming to the ridge, and for the first time Jeb was mad because she followed a slow trail. The wildcat crouched as if it were going to jump.

Jeb felt the horn. There was one way, he thought, to save the pup. He looked at the horn. One long blast and he knew Lucy would move over the ridge, coming to the sound. She was an old hound and had followed many trails. Once Jeb remembered Jeptha's saying that she was the only hound he would pit against a wildcat.

Jeb thought of the many days he had let the horn lie on the mantle while he had gone to the hillside garden. And he remembered why he had left the horn. But now, the white eye or stub tail of the pup no longer mattered. He knew he loved the small pup with all his might. The pup had found his trail and pushed his game like a true hound. It was Jeb who had failed. He knew that he could not blow the horn.

Tears welled in his eyes. Somewhere along the mountain, Jeb thought, Sampson once staggered. Maybe, Jeb thought, it was this same hollow. Sampson had found faith, enough faith to lift a whole mountain. Jeb looked again at the horn. It looked small compared to a mountain. He looked again toward the pup and the wildcat. Then he wiped his eyes and looked toward the moon.

"Lord," he said, "I know that that Book of Yours Grandma Quildy has is lots bigger than a box of doodlebugs. And I was ashamed of the pup You gave me, too. But I'm not ashamed any more. I haven't got the right to be a hunter, being that it takes a hunter to blow a horn. But if You are up there, Lord, like Grandma Quildy says, please let me blow it. I ain't got much time left and I got to call Lucy in."

Jeb raised the horn to his lips and took a deep breath. He blew with all his might. He blew until his face became red. And out of the end of the horn came nothing but wind. Trembling, Jeb pulled the horn from his lips.

"I ain't aiming to try and fool You this time, Lord," he said, and blew again.

The sweet music of the horn drifted through the deep woods and climbed the high ridge. And Jeb heard it echo over in the valley. And then the woods were quiet except for the whimper of the pup that had moved closer and the growl of the wildcat.

Through the brush came Lucy. She stopped in front of Jeb wagging her long tail. Then she sniffed the air and jumped at the whimper of the pup. She turned and leaped onto the back of the wildcat.

Over and over they went, first Lucy on top and then the wildcat. Lucy was grabbing for its throat and the wildcat was trying to

74

reach Lucy's stomach with its powerful claws. The pup jumped upon a ledge of the cliff and stood barking.

Lucy yelped and Jeb saw the red stream of blood come from her shoulder. The wildcat was on top now and Lucy fought to get up. Lucy yelped from the pain of the sharp claws.

The pup bawled into the air and with one long leap landed on the back of the wildcat. The pup rolled over and over on the ground, bouncing off the back of the wildcat. He had knocked the cat loose. The wildcat turned toward the pup. But before it could jump, Lucy had it by the throat. The pup ran around and around the wildcat, barking.

Finally Lucy let go of the wildcat and crawled away. And the wildcat lay still.

Jeb walked over and patted Lucy on the head. Her fur was covered with blood and Jeb wiped it with the sack he had tucked under his belt. Lucy licked his face as he lifted her in his arms and turned down the path that led out of the hollow. In front of him walked the small pup, his head high in the air. He stopped once, looked back at Jeb and Lucy and walked on. Jeb watched the short tail moving back and forth.

The steep walls of the valley were so tall that Jeb could not see the top. The woods were dark with the tall trees of the mountain. Even the small saplings that sprouted in the hollow were taller than Jeb. The horn bounced against his side and he touched it with his hand. Jeb looked again toward the moon and he felt as big as Sampson.

L O U I S   U N T E R M E Y E R

The Dog of Pompeii

Tito and his dog Bimbo lived (if you could call it living) under the
wall where it joined the inner gate. They really didn't live there;
they just slept there. They lived anywhere. Pompeii was one of the
liveliest of the old Latin towns, but although Tito was never an unhappy boy, he was not exactly a merry one.

The streets were always alive with shining chariots and bright
red trappings; the open-air theater rocked with laughing crowds;
sham battles and athletic sports were free in the great stadium.
Once a year the Caesar, or king, visited the pleasure city, and the
fireworks lasted for days; the ceremonies in the Forum were better
than a show.

But Tito saw none of these things. He was blind—had been blind from birth. He was known to everyone in the poorer quarters. But no one could say how old he was; no one remembered his parents; no one could tell where he came from.

Bimbo was another mystery. As long as people could remember seeing Tito—about twelve or thirteen years—they had seen Bimbo. Bimbo had never left the boy's side. He was not only dog, but nurse, pillow, playmate, mother, and father to Tito.

Did I say Bimbo never left his master? (Perhaps I had better say comrade. For if anyone was the master, it was Bimbo.) I was wrong. Bimbo did trust Tito alone exactly three times a day. It was a fixed routine, a custom understood between boy and dog since the beginning of their friendship, and the way it worked was this:

Early in the morning, shortly after dawn, while Tito was still dreaming, Bimbo would disappear. When Tito awoke, Bimbo would be sitting quietly at his side, his ears cocked, his stump of a tail tapping the ground, and freshly baked bread—more like a large round roll—at his feet.

Tito would stretch himself; Bimbo would yawn; then they would breakfast. At noon, no matter where they happened to be, Bimbo would put his paw on Tito's knee, and the two of them would return to the inner gate. Tito would curl up in the corner (almost like a dog) and go to sleep, while Bimbo, looking quite important (almost like a child), would disappear again. In half an hour he'd be back with their lunch. Sometimes it would be a piece of fruit or a scrap of meat. Often it was nothing but a dry crust. But sometimes there would be one of those flat rich cakes, sprinkled with raisins and sugar, that Tito liked so much.

At suppertime the same thing happened, although there was a little less of everything, for things were hard to snatch in the evening with the streets full of people. Besides, Bimbo didn't approve of too much food before going to sleep. A heavy supper made children too restless and dogs too stodgy—and it was the business of a dog to sleep lightly with one ear open and muscles ready for action.

But, whether there was much or little, hot or cold, fresh or dry, food was always there. Tito never asked where it came from and Bimbo never told him. There was plenty of rainwater in the hollows of soft stones; the old egg-seller at the corner sometimes gave Tito a cupful of strong goat's milk; in the grape season the boy ate plump grapes or drank their juice. So there was no danger of going hungry or thirsty. There was plenty of everything in Pompeii—if you knew where to find it—and if you had a dog like Bimbo.

As I said before, Tito was not the merriest boy in Pompeii. He could not romp with the other youngsters and play games like hare-and-hounds and I-spy and follow-your-master and jackstones and kings-and-robbers with them. But that did not make him sorry for himself.

If Tito could not see the sights that delighted the children of Pompeii, he could hear and smell things they never noticed. He could really see more with his ears and nose than they could with their eyes. When he and Bimbo went out walking, Tito knew just where they were going and exactly what was happening.

"Ah," he'd sniff and say, as they passed a handsome villa, "Glaucus Pansa is giving a grand dinner tonight. They're going to have three kinds of bread, and roast piglet, and stuffed goose, and a great stew—I think bear stew—and a fig pie." And Bimbo would note that this would be a good place to visit tomorrow.

Or, "Hmm," Tito would murmur, half through his lips, half through his nostrils. "Marcus Lucretius is expecting his mother. His servants are shaking out every piece of goods in the house; they're going to use the best clothes—the ones being kept in pine needles and camphor—and there's an extra servant in the kitchen. Come, Bimbo, let's get out of the dust!"

Or, as they passed a small but elegant dwelling opposite the public baths, Tito would say, "Too bad! The tragic poet is ill again. It must be a bad fever this time, for they're trying smoke fumes instead of medicine. Whew! I'm glad I'm not a tragic poet!"

Or, as they neared the Forum, Tito might say, "Mmmm! What good things they have in the marketplace today! Dates from Africa, and salt oysters from sea caves, and cuttlefish, and new honey, and sweet onions, and—ugh!—water-buffalo steaks. Come, let's see what's what in the Forum." And Bimbo, just as curious as his comrade, hurried on. Being a dog, he trusted his ears and nose (like Tito) more than his eyes. And so the two of them entered the center of Pompeii.

The Forum was the part of the town to which everybody came at least once during each day. It was the Central Square and everything happened here. There were no private houses; all were public

—the chief temples, the gold and red bazaars, the silk shops, the town hall, the booths belonging to the weavers and jewel merchants, the wealthy woolen market, the shrine of the household gods. Everything glittered here.

The buildings looked as if they were new—which, in a sense, they were. The earthquake over twelve years ago had brought down all the old buildings. Since the citizens of Pompeii were ambitious to rival Naples and even Rome, they had taken the opportunity to rebuild the whole town. And they had done it all within a dozen years. There was scarcely a building that was older than Tito.

Tito had heard a great deal about the earthquake, though being about a year old at the time, he could hardly remember it. This particular quake had been a light one—as earthquakes go. The weaker houses had been shaken down. Parts of the outworn walls had been wrecked; but there was little loss of life, and the brilliant new Pompeii had taken the place of the old.

No one knew what caused these earthquakes. Records showed they had happened in the neighborhood since the beginning of time. Sailors said that they took place to teach the lazy city folk a lesson. The ground shook to make people appreciate those who braved the dangers of the sea to bring them luxuries and protect their town from invaders.

The priests said that the gods took this way of showing their anger at those who refused to worship properly. The gods were most angry at those who failed to bring enough sacrifices to the altars.

The tradespeople said that the foreign merchants had corrupted the ground. They felt it was no longer safe to buy goods that came from strange places and carried trouble with them. Everybody had a different explanation—and everybody's explanation was louder and sillier than their neighbor's.

They were talking about it this afternoon as Tito and Bimbo came out of the side street into the public square. The Forum was the favorite promenade for rich and poor. The square was crowded to its last inch. There were priests arguing with politicians and servants doing the day's shopping. Tradespeople were crying their wares or displaying the latest fashions from Greece and Egypt. Children were playing hide-and-seek among the marble columns. And everywhere there were soldiers, sailors, and peasants from the provinces—to say nothing of those who merely came to lounge and look on.

Tito's ears even more than his nose guided him to the place where the talk was loudest. It was in front of the shrine of the household gods.

"I tell you," rumbled a voice which Tito recognized as bath-master Rufus's. "There won't be another earthquake in my lifetime or yours. There may be a tremble or two, but earthquakes, like lightning, never strike twice in the same place."

"Do they not?" asked a thin voice Tito had never heard. It had a high, sharp ring to it, and Tito knew it as the accent of a stranger. "How about the two towns of Sicily that have been ruined three times within fifteen years by the eruptions of Mount Etna? And were the people not warned? And does that column of smoke above Vesuvius mean nothing?"

"That?" Tito could hear the grunt with which one question answered another. "That's always there. We use it for our weather guide. When the smoke stands up straight, we know we'll have fair weather; when it flattens out, it's sure to be foggy; when it drifts to the east—"

"Yes, yes," cut in the edged voice. "I've heard about your weather guide. But the column of smoke seems hundreds of feet higher than usual, and it's thickening and spreading like a shadowy tree. They say in Naples—"

"Oh, Naples!" Tito knew this voice by the little squeak that went with it. It was Attilio, the cameo cutter. "*They* talk while we suffer. Little help we got from Naples the last time. Let them mind their own business."

"Yes," grumbled Rufus, "and others too."

"Very well, my confident friends," responded the thin voice which now sounded curiously flat. "We have a proverb—and it is this: Those who will not listen to humans must be taught by the gods. I say no more. But I leave a last warning. Remember the gods and goddesses. Look to your temples. And when the smoke tree above Vesuvius grows to the shape of an umbrella pine, look to your lives."

Tito could hear the air whistle as the speaker drew his toga about him, and the quick shuffle of feet told Tito the stranger had gone.

"Now what," said the cameo cutter, "did he mean by that?"

"I wonder," grunted Rufus.

Tito wondered too. And Bimbo, his head at a thoughtful angle, looked as if he had been doing a heavy piece of pondering. By nightfall the argument had been forgotten. If the smoke had increased, no one saw it in the dark. Besides, it was Caesar's birthday, and the town was in a holiday mood. Tito and Bimbo were among the merrymakers, dodging the charioteers who shouted at them. A dozen times the two almost upset baskets of sweets and fruits. And a dozen times they were cuffed. But Tito never missed his footing. He was thankful for his keen ears and quick instinct—most thankful of all for Bimbo.

They visited the uncovered theater. And though Tito could not see the faces of the actors, he could follow the play better than most of the audience, for their attention wandered. They were distracted by the scenery, the costumes, the by-play, and even by themselves. Tito's whole attention was centered in what he heard.

Then the boy and the dog went to the city walls where the people of Pompeii watched a mock naval battle. In it the city was attacked by way of the sea and saved after thousands of flaming arrows had been exchanged and countless colored torches had been burned. The thrill of flaring ships and lighted skies was lost to Tito. But the shouts and cheers excited him as much as any, and he cried out with the loudest of them.

The next morning there were *two* of the beloved raisin and sugar cakes for breakfast. Bimbo was unusually active and thumped his bit of a tail until Tito was afraid he would wear it out. The boy

The Dog of Pompeii   83

could not imagine whether Bimbo was urging him to some sort of game or was trying to tell something. After a while, he ceased to notice Bimbo. He felt drowsy. Last night's late hours had tired him. Besides, there was a heavy mist in the air—no, a thick fog rather than a mist—a fog that got into his throat and scraped it and made him cough.

Tito walked as far as the marine gate to get a breath of the sea. But the blanket of haze had spread all over the bay, and even the salt air seemed smoky.

He went to bed before dusk and slept. But he did not sleep well. He had too many dreams—dreams of ships lurching in the Forum, of losing his way in a screaming crowd, of armies marching across his chest, of being pulled over every rough pavement of Pompeii.

He woke early. Or, rather, he was pulled awake. Bimbo was doing the pulling. The dog had dragged Tito to his feet and was urging the boy along. Somewhere. Where, Tito did not know. His feet stumbled uncertainly; he was still half asleep. For a while he noticed nothing except the fact that it was hard to breathe. The air was hot. And heavy. So heavy that he could taste it. The air, it seemed, had turned to powder, a warm powder that stung the nostrils and burned his sightless eyes.

Then Tito began to hear sounds. Peculiar sounds. Like animals under the earth. Hissings and groanings and muffled cries that a dying creature might make dislodging the stones of its underground cave. There was no doubt of it now. The noises came from underneath. Tito not only heard them—he could feel them. The earth twitched. The twitching changed to an uneven shrugging of the soil. Then, as Bimbo half-pulled, half-coaxed him along, the ground jerked away from his feet and he was thrown against a stone fountain.

The water—warm water—splashing in his face revived him. He got to his feet, Bimbo steadying him, helping him on again. The noises grew louder; they came closer. The cries were even more animallike than before, but now they came from human throats. A few people, quicker of foot and more hurried by fear, began to rush by. A family or two—then no one—then, it seemed, an army broken out of bounds. Tito, bewildered though he was, could recognize Rufus as he bellowed past, like a water buffalo gone mad. Time was lost in a nightmare.

It was then the crashing began. First a sharp crackling, like a monstrous snapping of twigs; then a roar like the fall of a whole forest of trees; then an explosion that tore earth and sky. The heavens, though Tito could not see them, were shot through with continual flickerings of fire. Lightning above was answered by thunder beneath. A house fell. Then another. By a miracle the two companions had escaped the dangerous side streets and were in a more open space. It was the Forum. They rested here a while—how long Tito did not know.

Tito had no idea of the time of day. He could *feel* it was black —an unnatural blackness. Something inside—perhaps the lack of breakfast and lunch—told him it was past noon. But it didn't matter. Nothing seemed to matter. He was getting drowsy, too drowsy

The Dog of Pompeii 85

to walk. But walk he must. He knew it. And Bimbo knew it; the sharp tugs told him so. Nor was it a moment too soon. The sacred ground of the Forum was safe no longer. It was beginning to rock, then to pitch, then to split. As they stumbled out of the square, the earth wriggled like a caught snake, and all the columns of the temple of Jupiter came down. It was the end of the world—or so it seemed. To walk was not enough now. They must run. Tito was too frightened to know what to do or where to go. He had lost all sense of direction. He started to go back to the inner gate; but Bimbo, straining his back to the last inch, almost pulled his clothes from him. What did the creature want? Had the dog gone mad?

Then, suddenly, Tito understood. Bimbo was telling him the way out—urging him there. The marine gate, of course. The sea gate—and then the sea. Far from falling buildings, heaving ground. He turned, Bimbo guiding him across open pits and dangerous pools of bubbling mud, away from buildings that had caught fire and were dropping their burning beams. Tito could no longer tell whether the noises were made by the shrieking sky or the agonized people. He and Bimbo ran on—the only silent beings in a howling world.

New dangers threatened. All Pompeii seemed to be thronging toward the marine gate. And in squeezing among the crowds, there was a chance of being trampled to death. But the chance had to be taken. It was growing harder and harder to breathe. What air there was choked Tito.

It was all dust now—dust and pebbles, pebbles as large as beans. They fell on his head, his hands—pumice stones from the heart of Vesuvius. The mountain was turning itself inside out. Tito remembered a phrase that the stranger had said in the Forum two days ago: "Those who will not listen to humans must be taught by the gods." The people of Pompeii had refused to heed the warnings; they were being taught now—if it was not too late.

Suddenly it seemed too late for Tito. The red hot ashes blistered his skin, the stinging vapors tore his throat. He could not go on. He staggered toward a small tree at the side of the road and fell. In a moment Bimbo was beside him. He coaxed. But there was no answer. He licked Tito's hands, his feet, his face. The boy did not stir. Then Bimbo did the last thing he could—the last thing he wanted to do. He bit his comrade, bit him deep in the arm. With a cry of pain, Tito jumped to his feet, Bimbo after him. Tito was in despair, but Bimbo was determined. He drove the boy on, snapping at his heels, worrying his way through the crowd; barking, baring his teeth, heedless of kicks or falling stones. Sick with hunger, half dead with fear and sulphur fumes, Tito pounded on, pursued by Bimbo. How long he never knew. At last he staggered through the marine gate and felt soft sand under him. Then Tito fainted. . . .

Someone was dashing seawater over him. Someone was carrying him toward a boat.

"Bimbo," Tito called. And then louder, "Bimbo!" But Bimbo had disappeared.

Voices jarred against each other. "Hurry—hurry!" "To the boats!" "Can't you see the child's frightened and starving!" "He keeps calling for someone!" "Poor boy, he's out of his mind." "Here, child—take this!"

They tucked Tito in among them. The oarlocks creaked. The oars splashed. The boat rode over toppling waves. Tito was safe. But he wept continually.

"Bimbo!" he wailed. "Bimbo!" He could not be comforted.

Eighteen hundred years passed. Scientists were restoring ancient Pompeii. Excavators were working their way through the stones and trash that had buried the whole town. Much had already been brought to light. There were statues, bronze instruments, bright mosaics, household articles.

Even delicate paintings had been preserved by the fall of ashes that had taken over two thousand lives. Columns were dug up, and the Forum was beginning to take shape again.

It was a place where the ruins lay deepest that the Director paused now.

"Come here," he called to his assistant. "I think we've discovered the remains of a building in good shape. Here are four huge millstones that were most likely turned by slaves or mules—and here is a whole wall standing with shelves inside it. Why! It must have been a bakery. And here's a curious thing. What do you think I found under this heap where the ashes were thickest? The skeleton of a dog!"

The Dog of Pompeii 89

"Amazing!" gasped his assistant. "You'd think a dog would have had sense enough to run away at the time. And what is that flat thing he's holding between his teeth? It can't be a stone."

"No. It must have come from this bakery. You know it looks to me like some sort of cake hardened with the years. And, dear me, if those little black pebbles aren't raisins. A raisin cake almost two thousand years old! I wonder what made him want it at such a moment?"

"I wonder," murmured the assistant.

Part Three:

Where Foxes
and
Wolves Roam

WILLIAM J. FAULKNER

Brer Wolf's Magic Gate

In olden times in the Deep Woods, Brer Wolf and Brer Rabbit were neighbors.

So one day Brer Wolf said to Brer Rabbit, "Brer Rabbit, let's plant a garden."

Brer Rabbit shook his head. "I'm not going to plant any garden. The sun's too hot, and the ground's too hard. I'm not going to plant any garden."

Then Brer Wolf said, "Man, I'm going to put some collard greens and some turnips, cabbages, and carrots in my garden, and I'm going to have plenty to eat for the winter. You'd better not come there and try to get any of my vegetables."

"Man, I don't like those things. I eat the wild clover leaf myself," said Brer Rabbit.

Brer Wolf looked hard at Brer Rabbit, then went off to fix his garden. He marked off some land, and he dug in the ground, and he planted his collard greens, turnips, cabbages, and carrots, and he had a fine garden. And before he was through, he built a fence all around the garden, and he put a gate in the front. You could look through the gate, but you couldn't *get* through the gate. You see, Brer Wolf suspected that old Brer Rabbit might come to his garden and try to get some of his vegetables when he was asleep at night.

And sure enough, when the vegetables were all grown up and the collard greens looked nice through the gate, Brer Rabbit came sniffing around and made up his mind he was going to get some of that food. So one night, when the moon was shining bright and Brer Wolf was in the house a-snoring, Brer Rabbit crept toward the gate with a basket on his arm. When he came to the gate, he looked for the latch, but he couldn't find a latch. He looked for the hinges, but the gate didn't have any hinges.

Brer Rabbit said to himself, "Humph, this must be a magic gate. I'm going to hide myself here and wait till Brer Wolf comes back and see how he opens the gate." So Brer Rabbit got under the bushes and laid low until morning.

By and by old Brer Wolf came out to the garden gate, and he said to the gate, "Bubmeang! Bubmeang!" and the gate flew wide open. Then he went inside the garden and said to the gate, "Crimp up! Crimp up!" and the gate slammed shut. Brer Rabbit took out his little black notebook, and he wrote down the words, and he said, "He-he-he-he-he. I've got that. Now I know how to open that gate."

So the next night, when the moon was shining bright and Brer Wolf was in the house a-snoring, Brer Rabbit crept toward the gate again. And when he got close to the gate, Brer Rabbit took out his little black notebook and said, "How do you open the gate? Oh, yes, here it is." Then he said to the gate, "Bubmeang! Bubmeang!" and the gate flew wide open. When he got inside, he said to the gate, "Crimp up! Crimp up!" and the gate closed right up tight.

Then Brer Rabbit took out his knife, cut off the cabbages, cut down the collard stalks, and stuffed them in his basket. He pulled up the turnip greens, pulled up the carrots, and stuffed them in his basket. Then, when the basket was almost full, what do you think happened? Well, some clouds came right under the moon and shut out its light, and the garden was as black as midnight down in the swamp.

Brer Rabbit had to feel his way to the gate, and when he got there, he said, "How do you open the gate? I don't remember, and I can't see the words in my book. Oh, yes, I remember now." And he said to the gate, "Crimp up! Crimp up!" but the gate just said, "Bang, bang."

Hearing the bangs, Brer Wolf jumped out of bed, ran out on the piazza, jumped over the bannister, booketybook, booketybook, booketybook, and ran to the garden gate. "Who's that in my garden?" he called. "Who's that in my garden? I heard my gate slam."

Brer Rabbit stood there just a-trembling.

And then old Brer Wolf said to the gate, "Bubmeang! Bubmeang!" and the gate flew open just like that.

Brer Rabbit ran down to the bottom of the garden, lickety-split, lickety-split, and hid himself behind some collard stalks. And then what do you suppose happened? The clouds went right out from under the moon, and the garden was as bright as daylight again. And right in front of Brer Wolf was Brer Rabbit's basket, all full of vegetables.

"Ahuh, I know who was in my garden," said old Brer Wolf. "Nobody but that good-for-nothing rabbit. Come on out, Brer Rabbit. I'm going to get you, and when I do, I'm going to fix you good." And Brer Wolf walked around the garden, but he didn't see Brer Rabbit.

Brer Rabbit was still hiding behind the collard stalks, just a-trembling. And all the time Brer Wolf was getting closer and closer to Brer Rabbit, but he didn't see him. By and by, when old Brer Wolf got real close, Brer Rabbit got so scared that his ears popped straight up on his head.

Then Brer Wolf saw him, grabbed him by the leg, and laughed, "Ho-ho-ho-ho-ho. I've got you now, and I'm going to fix you good."

Brer Rabbit just laughed himself and said, "He-he-he-he-he. Brer Wolf, you surely are crazy."

"How come you say I'm crazy?" said Brer Wolf.

"Because you think you've got me by the leg when really you've got a collard stalk. How come you don't turn that collard stalk loose and grab me by the leg?"

Old Brer Wolf gasped in surprise. Then he turned Brer Rabbit's leg loose and grabbed the collard stalk. And Brer Rabbit ran out of the garden and down the road, lickety-split, lickety-split. And Brer Wolf never did catch him.

The Wolf

When the pale moon hides and the wild
    wind wails,
And over the treetops the nighthawk sails,
The gray wolf sits on the world's far rim
And howls: and it seems to comfort him.

The wolf is a lonely soul, you see,
No beast in the wood, nor bird in the tree,
But shuns his path; in the windy gloom
They give him plenty, and plenty of room.

So he sits with his long, lean face to the sky
Watching the ragged clouds go by.
There in the night, alone, apart,
Singing the song of his lone, wild heart.

Far away, on the world's dark rim
He howls, and it seems to comfort him.

Georgia R. Durston

MARIE HALUN BLOCH

The Foolish Dog and the Wolf
A Tale from the Ukraine

There was once a farmer's dog who came to believe that he lived a poor sort of life. Day and night he ran on the chain. Winter and summer he watched over the yard. For food, the mistress brought out a scrap of bread or a little soup. As for meat, only now and then did some trifle chance to fall his way. So he made up his mind to run off to the woods and live there in freedom.

One time, when the master had unchained him for the night, the dog took his chance and ran out of the farmyard. He roamed up and down the woods, whining for something to eat. But nothing chanced to come his way.

Along came a wolf. "Why are you roaming about here, Dog?" he asked.

"I'm looking for something to eat," the dog replied.

"All the food in the woods is mine!" the wolf cried. "Take yourself off!"

"But I've run away from my master," the dog said. "I no longer want to serve him, fighting all comers. I want to live in freedom."

"Well, in that case, come along with me," said the wolf. "I'll show you how to gain a living."

They went out of the woods into a field, and there some lambs were grazing. The wolf stood behind a bush and began to scrape up the earth with his front paws and to eat the dirt. As he ate, he asked the dog, "Is my fur beginning to bristle?"

"It is," the dog said.

"And my eyes—are they turning glassy?"

"They are."

"Very much?"

"No, not very much as yet."

The wolf pawed and ate more dirt. Then he asked, "And how now?"

"Oh," said the dog, "your fur is standing quite on end, and your eyes—it's frightful how glassy they've become!"

And it was true that the fur on the wolf's back was ruffled and his eyes had reddened.

Then the wolf hurled himself upon the lamb, and with one blow of his paw broke its back. He threw it over his shoulder and ran into the forest. Here he divided the meat with the dog and they had a fine, hearty meal.

Having eaten his fill, the dog thought, "Life in the woods is good! So much meat hasn't fallen to me in a whole year as I've eaten here in one meal. And it's not hard to come by! Why, don't I know how to scrape and eat dirt like the wolf? Only, the wolf is foolish: he steals a mere lamb—and how much meat do you get from a lamb? Why, I'll go at once and seize a horse!"

And he ran off to look for one. But the notion struck him that he needed a companion. Otherwise, who would look and tell him whether his fur had bristled and his eyes had turned glassy?

He had no sooner had the thought when lo! he saw a cat running about the woods. "And what, Kitten, are you doing here?" the dog asked.

"I'm hunting mice," the cat said.

"Eh, what sort of food is mice! Come along with me, I'll feed you with real meat!"

So the cat went along with him. They were coming out of the woods, when they spied a mare and her colt grazing in a meadow. The dog said, "There's my prey!"

With that he began to scrape the earth with his paws and to eat the dirt. As he ate, he asked the cat whether his fur was bristling and whether his eyes had turned glassy.

"No," the cat said. "Your fur is as before, and your eyes haven't turned glassy."

The dog scraped and ate more dirt and again asked, "And how now?"

"Same as before," the cat said. "Your fur isn't standing on end and your eyes haven't turned glassy."

The Dog flew into a rage. "You! Fool! Tell me that my fur is bristling and that my eyes are glassy," he instructed the cat, "for otherwise I won't catch the prey!"

Again the dog scraped the soil and ate. "Well?" he asked after a moment.

"Your fur is bristly," said the cat, "and your eyes are glassy."

With that the dog hurled himself upon the colt, meaning to bite through its throat. But the colt gave him a kick with its hoofs and the dog turned a somersault. The colt ran off.

The mare kept on grazing, from time to time glancing at the dog. And when he had come to his senses a little, she said, "You're a fool, Dog. Who ever heard of attacking a horse from the front? You have to do it from behind so that the horse won't notice. Now try eating me up from behind."

Glad for this sensible advice, the dog again began to scrape the soil and to eat it, all the while asking the cat whether his fur was standing on end and his eyes had turned glassy.

"On end," said the cat at last. "Glassy."

So the dog backed up and jumped at the mare from behind. She flashed out her hoofs and almost cracked his skull.

As the dog came tumbling down, the cat said, "Eh, brother, I see that your daily bread is hard to come by. I'd rather hunt mice."

With that, she left for the woods.

As for the dog, he lay in the meadow till evening, when his master found him, covered him, and carried him home.

PURA BELPRÉ

The Wolf, the Fox, and the Jug of Honey
A Tale from Puerto Rico

The Wolf and the Fox lived very near each other and they were the best of friends. The Fox had five little foxes, but the Wolf lived alone.

One day they went out for a walk, and on their way back, the Wolf stumbled over an earthenware jug almost hidden by the grass.

"Fox, stop and see what I found," he called.

But the Fox was worrying about her home and refused to stop. She called over her shoulder, "Leave it, Wolf, and come along."

"Come back, Fox," the Wolf pleaded, sniffing at the jug. "It's honey, a jug full of honey!"

"Honey? Are you sure? Well, well, that is a matter worth considering," said the Fox, joining her friend.

"Help me carry it home. It's much too heavy for me," said the Wolf.

"Home? Why can't we eat it here?" answered the Fox.

"I found it, didn't I?" asked the Wolf. "That makes it mine and I want to take it home."

"Then carry it yourself," said the Fox, and she started on her way again.

"Wait. Wait, Fox," called the Wolf. "I will share it with you if you help me."

"Very well," said the Fox, "I will."

As they walked home carrying the jug of honey, the Wolf proposed that the jug be kept untouched until he gave a dinner. Then they all would have honey for dessert.

"A very good idea," said the Fox.

When she reached home, however, she thought and thought of a plan to eat up all the honey before the Wolf decided on the dinner date. After a week of deep thinking, she called at the Wolf's home.

"Ay, *amigo* Wolf, I have been named godmother at a christening! Such a lovely feast will it be! Yet I will have to miss it."

"But why, *amiga* Fox?" asked the Wolf.

"My little foxes, *amigo*. They have to stay alone."

"Go, *amiga* Fox, go and have a good time. I will take care of them," said the Wolf.

So the Wolf came over to the Fox's home, and the Fox went over to the Wolf's home. She opened the jug and began to eat the honey. Late in the afternoon she returned.

"Did you have a good time, *amiga* Fox?" asked the Wolf.

"Fine! Fine!" answered the Fox, thinking how fine the honey had been.

"What name did you give the godchild?" he asked.

"Oh," answered the Fox, quickly, "Just Begun."

"Just Begun! What a queer name!" said the Wolf, as he returned home.

A week later, the Fox called again. She told the Wolf that she had been invited to another christening feast. She did not see how she could go. Yet . . .

"Oh, *amiga,* don't give it a thought. Of course you must go. A little relaxation is good for you," said the Wolf. "I will take care of your home."

So the Wolf came to the Fox's home, and the Fox went to the Wolf's home. She opened the jug of honey and started where she had left off the week before. When the sun went down, she returned home.

"Well, how did the christening go?" asked the Wolf.

"Sweet, simply sweet," answered the Fox, still enjoying the taste of the honey.

"What name did they give the godchild?" he asked again.

"Just Half, *amigo* Wolf, Just Half," she answered.

"What a strange name!" he said, as he returned home.

One morning the following week, the Fox arrived at the Wolf's home. *"Buenos dias, amigo,"* she said. "What a round of christenings are going on! This very morning . . ."

"If it's another invitation," interrupted the Wolf, "don't hesitate."

"Do you think I ought to go?" asked the Fox.

"Go, *amiga,* go. Never pass up a feast. I will take care of your home."

So the Wolf came over to the Fox's home, and the Fox went over to the Wolf's home, and ATE-UP-ALL-THE-HONEY. Early in the afternoon she arrived home, beaming with happiness.

"Aren't you a little early?" asked the Wolf. "Wasn't it a good christening feast?"

"Fine as usual, *amigo,*" said the Fox merrily. "Yet I don't think I'll be going to another for a long while."

"What name did they give the godchild?" asked the Wolf.

"Just Finished," answered the Fox, grinning. "A fine name!"

"I do not like it," said the Wolf, "but who am I to complain?" Discontentedly he walked home.

Time went by, and one day, as the two friends were walking along, the Fox remarked casually, "I have been patiently waiting for your dinner invitation. Times are bad, I know, so if you really can't afford it, let us forget all about it."

The Wolf was offended. "Can't afford it! Of course I can, and this very day." So he fixed a fine dinner, and the Fox and her five little foxes came over.

"Now for the dessert!" said the Wolf, when dinner was over. "Come, Foxes, give me a hand. It's a jug of honey!"

Up sprang the five little foxes. But in their excitement they stumbled over the jug, knocked it against the wall, and broke it into pieces. Poor little foxes! They looked up disappointedly. The jug was empty!

"Wolf," cried the Fox, "you have eaten up all the honey!"

"No! No!" cried the Wolf.

"Yes, yes!" cried the Fox.

"No honey!" cried the five little foxes.

"Hush! Hush!" ordered the Fox. "We will soon find out. He who eats honey always sweats honey, that is a fact. Let us take our siesta now, and we shall see what we shall see."

The Wolf and the five little foxes who had eaten so much fell asleep at once, but the Fox, who had eaten less, was wide awake. After a while she got up, and picking some of the broken pieces of jug, she came to the Wolf, who lay on his back sound asleep, and shook the last drops of honey left over his stomach. Then she lay down and waited for the Wolf to awake.

Pretty soon the Wolf stirred in his sleep and scratched his stomach. His paws stuck fast. Up jumped the Fox, crying, "So, *amigo* Wolf, you *are* sweating honey."

"Honey! Honey!" cried the five little foxes, waking up. They all sat on their haunches the better to watch the Wolf.

"I am sweating honey, indeed," exclaimed the Wolf. "Yet I can't remember having eaten it."

"Of course you can't, *amigo mio*. But you must have heard of people walking in their sleep. Who knows, *amigo*," said the Fox, sadly, "maybe you *are* such a one, a somnambulist."

GENEVIEVE BARLOW

The Fox and the Mole
A Tale Told in Peru

Once a fox and a mole were neighbors. Each lived in his own snug little cave at the foot of a rocky hill. Although their ways were quite different, they got along together very happily.

The fox was carefree, and spent his days roaming through the fields and forest in search of food and adventure. But the mole stayed close to home, and dug for worms that lay around the roots of plants growing near the caves.

One night, when the new moon cast a faint silver light over hill and fields, the fox visited the mole as he was sitting in front of his cave.

"What is your dearest wish, Mole?" asked the fox.

The mole answered promptly, "To have my pantry filled with those good worms that live around the potato roots. What do you wish for? Is it doves or partridges?"

"Nothing like that," the fox replied gaily. "I wish to get to the moon."

"To the moon?" the mole asked in astonishment, as if he did not hear correctly. "Did you say 'to the moon'?"

"Yes, to the moon. I would rather go there than travel to the sun or to the stars or roam the earth."

The mole shook his head in wonderment. "But how can you get there?"

"I wish I knew!" the fox said, with a deep sigh.

It was only a few days later, as the fox was tying a rope around a bundle of firewood, that a wonderful idea came to him. He shouted joyfully. "Now I know how to get to the moon! It's very simple. If I can get the condor to tie a rope to the tip of the moon, I can easily *climb* up there."

The fox picked up the firewood and rushed home. Excitedly, he called to the mole, "Good news! Come out and hear the good news!"

The mole appeared in his doorway. "What is it?"

"Tonight you and I are going to the moon. We will get the condor to help us!"

The mole hesitated for a moment, then inquired, "Will there be food for us on the moon?"

"Of course," the fox assured his neighbor.

"Then I will go," the mole answered.

"Wait here!" the fox commanded. He bounded toward the top of the hill, where the great condor lived.

"Good day, friend Condor," the fox called. "Will you help me?"

"Good day, Fox. Sit down, and tell me what you want me to do."

"Tonight Mole and I want to go to the moon, and you are the only one who can help us get there."

"I cannot carry you up there, because I am afraid to land on the moon."

"But would you be willing to fly near the moon?"

The condor nodded.

"Good!" said the fox. "Now I will get enough rope to reach the moon. Take one end of the rope in your strong beak, and fasten it securely to the tip of the new moon. Are you willing to do this?"

The condor agreed to the plan and said, "I shall begin my flight when I pick up the rope at your cave."

When darkness fell, the fox and the mole were impatiently waiting for the great bird. In front of the caves lay coils upon coils of strong rope made of the *cortadera* plant.

Finally, the condor arrived.

"All is ready," said the fox.

The condor took hold of the rope in his beak. As he flew, the rope rose up, up, up, higher and higher. The fox and the mole watched in awe. Finally, the condor returned from his long flight.

"The rope is tied securely," the condor reported. "But until you are on your way, I shall fly along with you."

The fox and the mole thanked the condor and made ready to start their climb.

The fox felt gay and fearless, but he knew Mole was nervous, so he said, "I shall go first so that I can warn you of any danger that may lie ahead."

"Good! But I am beginning to wonder if the food on the moon will be as good as it is here."

"Don't worry. It will be much better," the fox assured him cheerfully, as he started to climb up the rope.

The climbing fox was followed by the climbing mole. Up they went, paw over paw, paw over paw. Soon they were high above the treetops! Then they were looking down on the hill where they lived.

All at once they heard a loud, screeching "Ha, ha, ha!" It was the voice of a bright-colored parrot with beautiful green wings. It circled around them.

Thinking that the parrot was mocking them, the mole became angry. He stopped climbing, and shouted, "Be quiet, you clumsy, chattering longbeak. You are jealous because you cannot go to the moon."

Instead of answering, the parrot circled around and around the mole, each time coming closer.

"Silly nitwit, go back to earth. You will never get to the moon," the mole shouted.

"Ha, ha, ha! Neither will you!" the parrot replied, laughing.

Then the parrot flew to the rope above the mole's head. He began to peck, peck, peck with his sharp beak.

"Stop, stop!" pleaded the mole. "If you stop pecking at the

rope, I will give you enough corn to last a lifetime! White corn, yellow corn, purple corn, any color you wish!"

The parrot was too busy to answer.

"Peck, peck, peck." Then, CR-R-R-ACK, the rope broke.

The condor, flying beneath the mole, was prepared for this terrible moment. He caught the mole on his back, and flew him safely to his cave.

When the animals heard how foolish the mole had been, they began to taunt him and all his relatives. To avoid hearing these unkind remarks, all the moles left their dwellings in caves and rocks. They made homes for themselves beneath the earth. Since then they have lived in those burrows and come out only at night when the other animals are asleep.

And what happened to the fox? In Peru, it is said that on clear nights the fox can be seen standing on the moon and looking down on the earth.

And when the new moon appears, a bit of rope can still be seen dangling from the tip, if one looks very, very closely.

A Fox Jumped Up

A fox jumped up one winter's night,
And begged the moon to give him light,
For he'd many miles to trot that night
Before he reached his den O!
      Den O! Den O!

The first place he came to was a farmer's yard,
Where the ducks and the geese declared it **hard**
That their nerves should be shaken and their rest **so marred**
By a visit from Mr. Fox O!
      Fox O! Fox O!
That their nerves should be shaken and their rest **so marred**
By a visit from Mr. Fox O!

He took the grey goose by the neck
And swung him right across his back;
The grey goose cried out, "Quack, quack, **quack,"**
With his legs hanging dangling down O!
      Down O! Down O!

Old mother Slipper Slopper jumped out of bed
And out of the window she popped her head:
"Oh! John, John, John, the grey goose is gone,
And the fox is off to his den O!
       Den O! Den O!"

John ran up to the top of the hill,
And blew his whistle loud and shrill;
Said the fox, "That is very pretty music, still—
I'd rather be in my den O!
       Den O! Den O!"

The fox went back to his hungry den,
And his dear little foxes, eight, nine, ten;
Quoth they, "Good daddy, you must go there again,
If you bring such good cheer from the farm O!
       Farm O! Farm O!"
Quoth they, "Good daddy, you must go there again,
If you bring such good cheer from the farm O!"

The fox and his wife, without any strife,
Said they never ate a better goose in all their life;
They did very well without fork or knife,
And the little ones picked the bones O!
       Bones O! Bones O!
They did very well without fork or knife,
And the little ones picked the bones O!

Traditional

116   Part Three

SAM SAVITT

The Dingle Ridge Fox

The Dingle Ridge fox was asleep on a thick mat of October leaves, nesting snugly between the spreading roots of a great maple. He slept soundly with his nose and brush tucked together, but, like other creatures of the wild, his senses were sharply alert. The distant click of a steel-shod hoof striking stone penetrated his dreams and snapped him wide awake. He rose and stretched, listening hard as his nose tested the morning breeze.

A flock of crows lifted from the floor of the valley below and soared above him, squawking loudly as they flew by. Their warning was clear—it was time to get going.

The fox had spent a long night of hunting that had taken him far from his home grounds. But in the end, he had feasted on fresh-killed rabbit and afterward had enjoyed a most refreshing nap. Actually he preferred to travel after dark, but the sharp ring of the horseshoe plus the cry of the crows meant horses—and horses at this time of year usually meant hunters and hounds.

The fox trotted off, following the ridge line so he would be able to keep an eye on the valley. He was an old pro at fox hunting, at leading the hunt a merry chase through fields and woodland, over stone walls, and through swamps. He displayed enormous confidence in his ability to outlast any horse and outrace any hound. But lately the men had seemed to outguess every strategy he used.

Earlier that month a litter mate had been killed, and just four days ago the hounds had crossed his own line up near Duhollow and run him all the way to Starr Ridge, nearly five miles away. They almost got him then. The fox had heard the hounds crashing through the brush two jumps behind, but in the nick of time he reached a highway and shot across it through a stream of traffic and squealing brakes. He reached the far side unscathed and plunged into the woods below. Behind him he could hear howling cries and the huntsman's horn desperately calling in his pack.

Now, with the memory of that chase still fresh in his mind, the Dingle Ridge fox turned toward home.

At the bottom of a narrow gully he paused for a few quick laps of water, then bounded up a steep incline to a rock ledge where he stopped to listen once more. All was silent; then suddenly a hound yelped and the unmistakable beat of horses' hoofs vibrated across the land.

As yet the fox was not sure that he was the hunted. Also, he was not about to run across strange country in broad daylight if he could help it. But as he paused there, undecided, the voices of the hounds in full cry reached his ears and spurred him on up the slope. He gained the top and turned north, covering the ground at an easy lope. He was taking his time, saving his strength, for the day was young, the horses and hounds were fresh, and his den was many miles away.

Ordinarily the fox would have chosen a way that afforded the best cover, utilizing forest and wetlands to his advantage. But this was unknown territory, and the best thing to do right now was to get out of there as quickly as possible by the most direct route he could find.

The hounds came pouring up out of the gully behind him. They were really giving tongue now, for the scent was hot and their blood was up. From down below the huntsman's horn called, "Gone away, gone away!"

The huntsman came into view a moment later, mounted on a gray horse. His scarlet coat flashed in the sunlight as he galloped beside the hounds, cheering them on. In their wake the "field" appeared—a horde of riders, scarlet and black coated, leaning into the wind. Their horses were running flat out with their heads low and reaching, their hoofs ripping up huge clods of earth.

The land rolled on ahead in a series of yellowing fields separated by stone walls and rail fences. Cows looked up from their grazing to watch the fox go by. He moved straight as the flight of an arrow but veered left when he spotted a group of people standing on a high knoll to his right.

The terrain rose upward, then dipped sharply into a boulder-strewn valley of ditches and scrub growth. The fox could have circled it but he went right through the middle, running in a broken, zigzag line to slow his pursuers. A shallow brook crossed in front of him and he turned with it, bounding through the water for almost three hundred yards before he leaped up on the bank.

He stood there a moment listening, to see if he had succeeded in throwing the hounds off his trail. But all he had managed to do was slow them down. Brewster, a big black-and-tan veteran of many a hunt, seemed to pick his scent out of the air. His voice cried, "This way, this way!" Seconds later, a full chorus joined in and the pack was off and running once more.

For the next hour the fox employed every tactic he knew to shake off the hounds. He was hampered by the unfamiliar country, but as a resourceful, intelligent animal he was quick to make the most of every opportunity that presented itself. He splashed across swamps and scooted along the tops of stone walls. When he chanced upon a cowbarn, he darted right through the middle of it, to the utter surprise of a farmer standing in the hayloft, then plunged through the manure pile as he left. At one time he walked slowly in amongst a flock of sheep, careful not to alarm them, for he knew their droppings would obliterate his scent. They did, but the wily huntsman regrouped his baffled pack and cast them again where he reckoned their quarry would have come out.

As the fox cut through the back yard of a farmhouse, a pair of small terriers gave chase, yapping at his heels. He paid little attention to them, for they were accomplishing the same purpose as the sheep by mingling their scent with his.

Half a mile later, the fox happened on the track of another fox. He stayed right on it for a short while, then leaped to the top of a boulder and changed his direction, expecting the hounds to stick to the other scent.

But none of these strategies seemed to slow up the pursuers. The huntsman knew his business. He controlled and deployed his pack with an uncanny skill that brought them closer and closer to their prey. On the banks of Titicus Lake, almost six miles south of Dingle Ridge, he pulled up to give his horse a breather. The animal's flanks were heaving and his gray coat was dark with sweat.

He pranced and tossed his head, throwing huge hunks of froth back at his rider.

The master of the hunt rode up alongside the huntsman. "My horse has thrown a shoe, Jack," he announced. "I'd better pull out before he goes lame."

A good part of the field, feeling that their horses had had enough, followed the master home, but six decided to stay on to the end.

The hounds had lost the scent. They scurried along the shore of the lake, whining and yipping with anxiety. The huntsman surmised the fox had turned either right or left, using the shallow water to obscure his trail.

Suddenly somebody yelled, "Tally ho—there he goes!"

Across the lake the hunters could see the fox just making shore. They watched as he stood there for a moment, dripping wet. Then the fox shook himself and, climbing the far bank, disappeared into the heavy growth beyond.

The huntsman hurriedly gathered his hounds and sent them in a mad rush around the lake. Spray and mud flew from the horses' hoofs as they galloped along the bank to the point where the fox had vanished.

The hounds picked up the scent with a howling outcry. They scuttled through a four-rail fence and the huntsman's gray jumped it boldly, going away. The following horse chopped out the top rail and turned over, throwing his rider. The animal immediately lunged to his feet and followed the others as they went flying by. The horseless rider staggered after him shouting, "Whoa! Whoa!"

But there wasn't a chance in the world that his mount would stop.

The cold swim had refreshed the tired fox. He reached the railroad tracks that pointed north and loped along them to the trestle that spanned the town sprawled out below. He slowed to a walk and crossed the long expanse, stepping gingerly on each rail tie until he made the far side.

The huntsman, far ahead of the others, sighted the fox when the animal was almost halfway over. He blew in his hounds and skirted the town, with the field of five riders and one riderless horse nearly a half mile behind.

From the beginning he had suspected their quarry was the Dingle Ridge fox but now he was certain of it. He had hunted foxes for years. He knew all about them, their habits and their strategies. But no fox he had ever known was more daring or more ingenious than this one.

By the time the hounds reached the north end of town, their prey was well on his way to Dingle Ridge.

The hunters settled into their saddles for the last lap of the race. They were bone weary, and their muscles cried out against the steady pounding. Their horses were lathered and blowing hard, and the hounds, still running on ahead with the huntsman, were tiring rapidly.

At Duhollow Junction the fox had been running for more than two hours. His red coat was all scuffed and flecked with mud and his tongue hung almost to the ground. Only his tail still managed to stay aloft like a banner, defiant to the end. He was truly close to exhaustion—but so were his pursuers.

At last he was on familiar ground. Before him spread a golf course where horsemen would not dare to follow. Beyond that between him and Dingle Ridge ran the highway.

He was moving much more slowly now, for the pace was beginning to tell. The pride in his speed had withered away and his lungs, laboring painfully, seemed grown old.

His earliest training had taught him never to leave a straight trail if a crooked one was at all possible. But under the present circumstances, a straight line was the shortest distance between himself and home. He crossed the golf course in this manner, looking neither right nor left and paying no attention to the golfers staring at him as he went by.

There was no time to look back, and he was concentrating only on that which was up front. The fox had almost reached the edge of the golf course when the hounds emerged from the woods and swept onto the green. Their cries surged through the fox like fresh blood to give him a new spurt of energy and the feeling that all was not yet lost.

The huntsman checked his horse at the edge of the velvet turf and sized up the situation instantly. The Dingle Ridge fox was leading the pack to the highway again and disaster. He circled the course at a dead gallop in an effort to head them off.

He caught up with the hounds on the far side and managed to call in most of them. But Brewster and some of the leaders had already crossed over.

The fox knew where he was going now. The closeness of his goal renewed his flagging strength. His pace picked up as he sprinted through a grove of trees and fairly flew into a rocky ravine that wound its way up a jagged slope through an impenetrable mass of windfalls and tangles of vines that would stop the horses—but not the pack.

As the hounds lunged up the draw, closing on the fox, all that could be heard was their panting breaths for they had no wind left to give tongue.

Near the top, the fox turned into the dense undergrowth. Soon in front of him a huge stone wall rose out of the gloom. It had probably been built there when the forest was a clearing over a hundred years before. But the rains and snows of countless seasons had eroded the earth on either side of it and what had started out as a four-foot wall was now almost seven feet high. The trees and vegetation pressing inward had kept it from crumbling. The wall itself was impossible to scale, but several months before the fox had discovered a narrow tunnel at its base just about wide enough to accommodate him in a pinch.

The lead hound snapped his jaws on empty air as the fox dove into the shaft and frantically squirmed his way through. The hound's head followed him in but his shoulders slammed against the sides, stopping him cold. He howled with frustration and began digging madly—but the chase was over.

The fox was safe at last. He crouched against the far wall until he heard the horn calling off the hounds. Afterward he stretched out on his side with his flanks pulsating against the cool earth.

He stayed where he was for the remainder of the day, waiting for his vitality to return. Shortly after dusk he rose to his haunches. He felt sore and stiff but mostly hungry. He quenched his thirst at a nearby stream, then moved up out of the woodland.

The night was cold. An enormous orange moon climbed above the treetops to shed a soft warm light over the countryside. The fox stalked along an old cowpath to a wide grassy meadow where he knew of a hollow overgrown with coarse grass, the playground of a colony of field mice. He sat next to it and waited. Presently a faint squeak showed that the game was astir. The fox rose up on tiptoe, not crouching but as high as he could stand so as to get a better view. The runs that the mice followed were hidden under the grassy tangle and the only way to know the whereabouts of a mouse was by seeing the slight shaking of the grass and pouncing instantly upon it. The trick was to locate the mouse, seize him first, and see him afterward.

A half-dozen mice served as an adequate appetizer. Just before dawn, the fox located a white rooster asleep on top of a farmyard fencepost, and that completed his meal for the night.

As the sun came up in the east, the Dingle Ridge fox crawled into his den, well hidden beneath a rocky ledge. Inside he circled once or twice, then collapsed into a deep bed of leaves. His nose snuggled into the warmth of his luxurious tail as he slept, and as he dreamed his legs jerked spasmodically and twitched from time to time.

PART THREE

All the following week the fox moved restlessly through the area, mostly at night. He hunted and ate and slept but did not stray far from his home base. Sometimes he amused himself by trying to catch frogs in a pond below his den. More often he sat in the shelter of a spreading barberry bush, watching the cows graze in the valley or a redtail hawk rising and gliding against the autumn sky.

He could not help but be aware that during the past few years most of the foxes had left his part of the country and drifted toward the mountains where horses and hounds could not follow. The urge to go with them was in him, but he hung back—waiting for he knew not what.

One Saturday morning the fox turned north toward the high country. Last night a vixen had called from up there, and perhaps the time had come to move in that direction, where he would be safe.

Just as he was about to enter the forest, the long wavering notes of a hunting horn floated up to him. He turned and listened. The sound came again from the valley far below. It made his heart quicken and the blood within him sing. He crouched at the brink of a grassy ledge where he could get a better view.

He saw the hunt gathering. Instantly he picked out the huntsman on his gray horse with the hounds milling around—whining, yelping, anxious to be on their way. They began moving off, the huntsman and hounds up front with the field falling in behind.

The Dingle Ridge fox rose to his haunches. He paused there for a second, then flew down the long slope, zigzagging his way through brush and boulders. At the foot of the steep incline he angled across a wide meadow, running easily downgrade.

As the sound of the hunting horn echoed once more, the fox increased his pace. He knew that just ahead, and to his right, hounds were seeking a fox. If he hurried they would cross his line for another exciting race with death.